MW00585584

By Sarah Manguso

FICTION

Liars
Very Cold People
Hard to Admit and Harder to Escape

NONFICTION

300 Arguments
Ongoingness
The Guardians
The Two Kinds of Decay

POETRY

Siste Viator
The Captain Lands in Paradise

LIARS

LIARS

a novel

Sarah Manguso

HOGARTH
NEW YORK

Published in the United States by Hogarth, an imprint of Random House, a division of Penguin Random House LLC, New York.

HOGARTH is a trademark of the Random House Group Limited, and the H colophon is a trademark of Penguin Random House LLC.

Portions of this work were originally published in "Love" by Sarah Manguso in *Pets: An Anthology,* edited by Jordan Castro (New York: Tyrant Books, 2020).

LIBRARY OF CONGRESS CATALOGING-IN-PUBLICATION DATA
Names: Manguso, Sarah, author.
Title: Liars: a novel / by Sarah Manguso.
Description: First edition. | New York: Hogarth, 2024.
Identifiers: LCCN 2023033510 (print) | LCCN 2023033511 (ebook) | ISBN 9780593241257 (Hardback) | ISBN 9780593241264 (Ebook)
Subjects: LCGFT: Novels.
Classification: LCC PS3613.A54 L53 2024 (print) | LCC PS3613.A54 (ebook) | DDC 811/.6—dc23/eng/20230724
LC record available at https://lccn.loc.gov/2023033510
LC ebook record available at https://lccn.loc.gov/2023033511

Printed in the United States of America on acid-free paper

randomhousebooks.com

2 4 6 8 9 7 5 3 1

First Edition

Book design by Susan Turner

LIARS

In the beginning I was only myself. Everything that happened to me, I thought, was mine alone.

Then I married a man, as women do. My life became archetypal, a drag show of nuclear familyhood. I got enmeshed in a story that had already been told ten billion times.

But before all that, back at the beginning, I remember looking out the door of my apartment, watching John's head appear as he climbed the stairs, and then, step by step, more and more of him.

Which is when I said, *You're real!*

Which was my first mistake.

Upstate for the summer, I was house-sitting and making vigorous use of the fireplace. I walked by the Hudson and sometimes swam. The locals said that you could pick through the river bottom and find pure garnets, but I never found any, so I tried to write poems about not finding them.

I pretended that the house was mine, and that I'd paid it off and lived alone. I pretended I was fifty years old and had published many books translated into many languages. I imagined seducing the beautiful young men who installed satellite dishes and fixed cars and lived in my neighbors' converted stables.

The house didn't have a satellite dish, and the only theater in town screened Hollywood fluff that had played in the city months earlier, but in late June a film festival came to town.

The reception after opening night was the first party I'd attended in a long time, and I introduced myself to the Canadian filmmaker whose film had been my favorite. The action took place at the foot of a mountain over hundreds of years. The last shot was just the landscape. It was calm and forthright. It resembled him. His name was John.

He and I drank two drinks together, and then I followed him to his room in the inn, where I saw all the things he'd collected over his three days in town. Mugs with dried red wine at the bottom, or half an inch of milky old coffee. Overdue books from the New York Public Library, river stones, castoffs from a local flea market, and all the birch bark he'd found on the ground all week, apparently—it was everywhere. I hadn't picked up any of it. Because it was everywhere.

It was dark, and I was afraid of the dark—the real dark, the country dark. It isn't dark in the city even though we refer to dark alleys and dark nightclubs. Those are only *city* dark. In the country, under the right circumstances of moon and weather, the dark can be depthless. I had never seen this dark before, but John was from Alberta and didn't mind it. In fact he seemed to love it. I didn't hold his hand in the dark, that first night, but I took his arm, and he led me back to my little house in the night.

Over the next week he hand-delivered a birch-bark note to me in my mailbox every day, and halfway through that week we started fucking and didn't stop for almost fifteen years.

I tried to understand that first ferocious hunger and couldn't. It came from somewhere beyond reason.

He had the calm, unguarded eyes of someone who had already seen everything. Those eyes, his heavy limbs, the raucous black bloom of pubic hair. He smelled like cedar. I asked him whether this happened to him often, because it hadn't ever happened to me. *Not like this,* he said.

He said that in the next two years he wanted to make a name for himself, put his finances in order, and find gallery representation for his photographs. I wanted to publish a book-length poem and get a tenure-track teaching job.

He wanted to win the Akadimía Prize, which would take him to Athens, Greece, for a year, to live in a beautiful villa and work in an airy studio and eat food prepared by chefs.

He said that I should apply, too—every year the fellowships were given to two artists, two writers, two architects, two medievalists, and so on.

I felt dull when I remembered that John could write, draw, and make photographs and films, while I could only write. I wondered if I'd feel like a failure next to him. But then I remembered that he thought clearly, felt deeply, worked hard, made art, was dark and handsome, and wanted to marry me. I'd ordered à la carte and gotten everything I'd wanted.

He said he'd dated two women at once, one year, and that they'd found out about each other.

He said that his last relationship had died a slow death and ended in guarded friendship, but I knew it might yet be there, steering him.

He said he'd known right away that he'd spend the rest of his life with me. Then he said, *That's what's called showing one's hand, or putting all one's cards on the table,* and then I said, *I'll totally marry you.*

———

Back in the city, where we both lived, providentially on the same subway line, we visited each other's apartments. His was in a cruddy row house in a neighborhood that hadn't been gentrified yet; all his neighbors were in their eighties. His apartment, a top floor walk-through, was dotted with glass vases from rummage sales, stones and seashells, an old edition of Poe nibbled beautifully by bookworms. He crouched next to some bookshelves he'd made and plugged something into the wall outlet and then looked up at me. In a translucent orange vase the size of a pineapple, a ball of wadded-up Christmas lights was suddenly aglow.

John said that we had to be discreet while walking in his neighborhood. He hadn't told his ex-girlfriend about me, and I said that that wasn't good enough, and he listened to me and then rescinded the rule.

But Naomi still called him every night. He claimed she was suicidal and that it was his responsibility to save her.

She's . . . unstable, he said, the little pause making the second word even darker, more dangerous.

I said that he was valuing her feelings above mine. I said that she couldn't control our relationship with her phone calls and suicide threats, and I asked John to limit his communication with her.

I couldn't sleep unless no one was touching me, but John couldn't sleep unless he was holding on to me. Tight.

I wish I were more like you, he said.

Then I found his Friendster profile, which he'd logged into within twenty-four hours, and which listed him as thirty-four and single.

My mother said that John wasn't ready to settle down right away because he hadn't expected to meet me.

Then John emailed me and said that Naomi had found out about me, that she would come over that weekend for the final breakup, after which he'd change his profile.

I wrote back, *I'm not going to have a meltdown and break up with you. You're going to have to work consistently and effortfully to sabotage this. It's not impossible, but I don't think you have the heart to do it. At least I really, really hope you don't.*

I signed it, *I love you, Mumbun. Mumbun,* our pet name for each other, derived very early on from *Bunny*. John, my tender arctic hare.

That night he visited, heartbroken over something else—a friend had lost his dead father's jigsaw and bought him a used one to replace it, even though he'd requested that she buy a new one, and then she'd lied and said he'd never said it. I petted him and massaged his back and listened to his sadness, and I sensed that he was learning.

The next morning he sexily disassembled my old inkjet printer, looking for parts he could use to make a robot for a photography project. I was revising a book review. It was late morning when the mail came. Mostly junk. Two magazines. A letter.

I put the magazines on the desk, put the junk mail in the bin under the kitchen sink, and opened the letter from the Akadimía. When I read that I'd won the Akadimía Prize I went cold, knowing I'd have to conceal my pride when I told John. Affectless, he said, *I want to be as successful in my field as you are in yours.* Then he put down his little tools and took me out for brunch. We waited forty minutes for a table while we both stewed, him about not having won the photography fellowship, me about wishing we'd eaten oatmeal at home for free.

Fifteen years earlier, when I'd gone away to college, I wore a fur coat I'd bought for ten dollars at a thrift store. It was Persian lamb, the fur rotting off the skin. I used reeking permanent black markers to color in the skin as the fur fell off. My mother had showed me how to do it.

I sang in the choir; that was six hundred dollars a semester. I was a research assistant for a doctoral student; that was eleven dollars an hour. I shelved books at the music library in the afternoons; that was minimum wage, four twenty-five.

One night in the dining hall I'd bumped into a classmate who worked in the kitchen. I spilled my plastic cup of grape juice all over his white chef's jacket. I wanted to pay for the cleaning, but the jacket would just go into the institutional wash. I'd needed to pay for something, though. I'd felt guilty for having any money at all.

When one day someone casually referred to my tony Manhattan girls' school, I proudly told him I'd gone to public school in Massachusetts. He seemed impressed that I could play rich so convincingly. He was from Ohio. I was a liar, but I didn't know it yet.

John and I went together to the first meeting of that year's class of Akadimía Fellows. All around the big table stood chairs at equal intervals, with stacks of paper in front of each one. John sat down next to me. The other spouses and partners all sat in the chairs against the wall.

Mortified, I didn't say anything. I didn't want to insult John. *A seat at the table is too much to ask?* he would have said. *But none of the other fellows' partners are at the table,* I would have said. Then he would have said it wasn't worth discussing, a man sitting in one chair when he could have been sitting in a different one, why was I making it an issue, what was wrong with me. John would do what he wanted, I was crazy, he was the partner of a crazy person. Whom he loved anyway, dearly.

That night he went out and didn't call and came home late. In the morning he said he'd *gone out drinking,* a phrase that repelled me. I hated the person John became when he drank, tormented by the idea that he wasn't smart enough, able only to regale everyone about how bright a student he'd once been.

He had a hangover and didn't remember what he'd said to his graduate students, but he'd probably gossiped about his colleagues again while the students tittered. When I told him he had to stop doing that, he laughed at me.

In September, I packed three suitcases and moved to Greece and became an Akadimía Fellow at the Amerikanikí Akadimía in Athens. John stayed in New York for a couple of months, working and saving money and, I hated myself for thinking it, brooding about not having won the prize. One night my neck and shoulders were so tense, I needed a massage so desperately, that several other fellows came to visit me in my apartment in the villa. They rubbed my neck and spoke kindly to me.

Each morning, after I showered and dressed and colored in my patchy eyebrows with a pencil, I went downstairs to the coffee bar. The barman was capable of communicating entire sentences using just his eyes. His mouth never moved. He knew I wanted a makiáto before I was capable of waking sufficiently to speak Greek or any other language.

He called out the names of those who dared to keep their coffee on the bar for more than ten seconds, after which the particulate begins to drift toward the bottom of the cup and the shot is ruined. I always jumped up to seize mine, hurried to it like a wife. After drinking it I gave the barman a two-euro coin and he snapped my change onto the marble bar—usually something between thirty and forty cents even though I always bought the same coffee and bougatsa. When I got fifty cents back one morning I thought he must approve of me.

When John arrived it was almost winter. I led him through the entrance and past the fountain and up the marble steps. Then I dragged open the massive iron gate and we walked into the courtyard. John looked around and I watched him take it all in. Thousand-year-old stones were mounted in the ochre walls. It was a second layer, a higher level, of knowing the place. *Whoa,* he said. It fed me. We'd been together a year.

———

John sulked, fixated on his unsuccessful fellowship applications. *Maybe I can't be a mellow, easygoing guy and also an art star,* he said.

In the beginning, everything about him had shone, but as time passed, I noticed that he used the word *phenomena* as a singular noun, couldn't spell the word *necessary,* couldn't write a coherent paragraph. Next to him, I was brilliant. Next to me, he was beautiful, charming, and initially capable of hiding all the things that, in my wrinkly little heart, made me consider him inferior.

I lay in bed naked, and John sketched me all day long, with encounters every now and then. I came in his mouth, rode him, and let him pull my hair, then came again in his hand just as he came in my mouth. At the end of the day he asked, *Do you think we could get into that marriage column in* The New York Times?

At dinner, the painter said, *You seem like a completely different person now that John's here. It makes me think that you have a good relationship.*

Without meaning to, I began to restrict the material in my diary. I had become unable to articulate certain feelings. And so my body became their cultivation dish.

After we took care of the painter's baby for the afternoon, the painter's wife said to me, *I don't know how many points you give for good-with-kids, but John gets them all.*

That night John said, *Is it a comfort to you that I've always assumed we'd get married?* but a moment later he said he didn't want to be the unsuccessful partner of the successful person. Then he apologized and said that he'd just wanted to be honest. I said, *It was brave and considerate to tell me.*

I signed up for extra Greek conversation lessons with a couple of the other fellows. John had been skipping the regular classes. When I told him I'd signed up for another round of lessons without him, he sat and cried silently without moving his face. Tears dripped from his jaw. I was surprised.

That night there was a dance party. I left at one in the morning. John said he'd stay another fifteen minutes, but he stayed three more hours. In the morning he seemed contrite and frightened.

A week later, the photography fellow showed photos from the party, including two of John and a classicist posing as if they were about to make out. In shock, I asked John how he would feel if he were me. *Sad, hurt, angry,* he said.

God, but he was funny. The painter's wife was pregnant again, and we all signed a card. John wrote, *Good luck! The last time I had a baby they still let you drink and gamble in the delivery room. I was so doped up I bet on the Cleveland Browns to win the Kentucky Derby.*

Every now and then one of the fellows was invited to give a talk or mount a show in Spain or Germany or Slovenia. The painter and his wife were trying to decide whether to leave the Akadimía for a research trip to Morocco. The wife wasn't sure she wanted to go. *We're a team,* the painter said to her. She and the baby went with him.

My best friend Hannah was married to her first husband for thirteen years. We met after I sent her a fan letter through a magazine editor, and we became best friends immediately.

One night we went to a party, Hannah and her husband and I, and she left before we did. While her husband and I waited for a bus home, he lit a cigarette. He smoked half of it, dropped it, sprayed his mouth with mint spray, unwrapped and chewed a piece of gum, took a little bottle of hand sanitizer out of his coat, and rubbed it all over his hands and forearms in front of me so that we'd have a secret. Testing me to see if I'd lie for him.

Hannah finally divorced him while I was in Greece. She knew so much more than I did about being with a man. Nothing I told her ever shocked her. The contours of her life lay beyond the outer limits of mine. She sublet my apartment while I was gone, and she reminded me constantly that my life with John was normal.

At lunch John trash-talked James Joyce, as he often did when he despaired that his work didn't sufficiently represent him in the world. Then he walked into town with some of the other fellows. I didn't want to go. *We're a team,* he said, and then went without me.

Instead of calling me and telling me where to meet them for dinner, he emailed from a kiosk, but I didn't have email that day because he'd used my IP address to download a movie and we'd been kicked off the server for using too much data. My screaming heart told me that John had pretended to try to reach me but really just wanted to hurt me. I spent three hours worried sick, and then the restaurants all closed and I had nothing for dinner.

I made up the foldout bed in my studio.

John woke me at two in the morning, and we fought in screaming whispers. At four I went back to the dorm, nauseated. John hugged onto me right away and fell asleep. In the morning he left without telling me where he was going. Treading water, awaiting death—how interesting, the future had disappeared. I wondered what would happen next.

On the night of my birthday I sat at a white-draped table at the Akadimía and thought, *Maybe someone will stick a candle in my kassato*. Then the lights dimmed. Everyone looked up. Into the dining room John and the chefs wheeled a trolley bearing a massive frosted cake. Six months into a ten-month fellowship, no one had ever had a birthday cake. Everyone sang. By morning we heard that the director was furious that John hadn't asked permission to hijack the kitchen. It didn't matter. Everyone in the kitchen loved him.

While we all ate the cake, the filmmaker said that he'd known he couldn't afford a nice ring, so he'd just bought a cheap one and took his wife out to lunch after their courthouse wedding.

That night John and I sat in bed and wrote and sketched in our little books, having tuned out everything including each other, but just having him there, next to me, seemed to calm my autonomic nervous system. I loved it.

John said, *We've had a lot of external validation this year that we work well as a couple.*

I didn't want to give up my apartment back home until we were really engaged, so John said, *My beloved, will you marry me?* And I said yes. And that I didn't need an expensive ring.

He said we'd be engaged, for real, by Christmas. He said that the only reason we weren't engaged was that he couldn't afford a ring. Then he arranged to get six more shirts made.

On the day before we flew home, after a steamy walk back to the villa in the height of the Athenian summer, John and I quarreled. I accused him of contradicting everything I said just for the sake of it. As after every quarrel, we then examined and speculated on our friends' relationships, describing lovingly to each other their myriad flaws.

Then I got into the fountain in my black dress and floated on my back and watched the fast clouds in the dark sky. John watched me swim and laugh. I prayed to remember the joy of that moment until the end of my life.

Back home in New York, we threw a party. John's ex-girlfriend Naomi showed up in a backless evening gown and no bra. She stood much too close to John, gazing into his eyes and brushing against his body at every opportunity.

Just let this be her problem, John said later. *She's not going to stop until you set a boundary,* I said. *I love you, and I don't want needless obstacles getting in the way of my love.*

The next day he wrote me a note. *I will actively work on this. Thank you for telling me. I don't ever want you to doubt that you are my love. Because you are.*

I grew up half crazy, living with people who were more than half crazy, and I left home and paid for ten years of psychotherapy and chose the wrong people, over and over, and if they were any good I left them because I thought I deserved only ruined people, and that to be alone was my destiny, and I never shared my home with a partner until I was thirty-four and moved in with a man who'd said he would propose to me by Christmas, and I believed him because we'd been together two years, and I loaned him eight thousand dollars for a film and he didn't propose to me by Christmas, and then I turned thirty-five.

Still owing me eight thousand dollars, John asked for more. My shame felt like a fever. He said he'd ask his mother for some money. Then he ordered a two-hundred-dollar lamp.

Alone in a hotel in a faraway town for a poetry reading, I took a bath, rubbed one out, slept alone in a giant bed, and relaxed for the first time in weeks.

Then I realized that I liked to work when John wasn't there.

Then I realized that without John, I had more fun at parties.

The night I got home, during sex John slapped my face playfully but too hard and I erupted, sobbing, as surprised as he looked. Afterward, almost asleep, I heard myself say, *You're the best thing that's ever happened to me.*

In the morning I bought a used cream-colored silk dress for fifty-five dollars to get married in.

And then one night John made a reservation at the oyster bar for no discernible reason.

We took the train to the Village and climbed the stairs. It was so cold. We turned left onto a twisty street, and in front of my favorite haunted house, John stopped.

He said, *Uh, I guess this is as good a moment as any to ask you to be my wife.* But we'd already agreed that I'd become his wife. He wasn't looking at me. He sounded detached and frightened. I was laughing, trying to encourage him. I was happy, grinning. I wanted this part of my life to be over already, and I was so glad that it finally was.

I looked down at the ring. The little diamond was gray and tear-shaped. I loved it. I put it on, and it was too big.

Then we walked the rest of the way to the restaurant and sat down and immediately ordered prosecco. John toasted, *Here's to every other day.*

At last I was ready to give up my apartment. As we packed my things, a framed picture fell to the floor. The glass shattered. I went to the kitchen for a paper bag, dustpan, and brush. We swept up the broken glass. When we finished, John said, *Being an adult is really annoying,* trying for levity. Had he never swept a floor? I tucked away the little shard of the day because I couldn't imagine that it could be true, that he would actually think what he appeared to be thinking.

I moved into John's apartment and decided to tidy up. With his permission I sorted through the three drawers of his metal filing cabinet and gathered up all the old utility bills and brought them to the office supply store to be shredded.

I found the letter he'd written to the deans of his college after they'd declined his application to study abroad. I read their letters, too. I gave him the letters in a neat stack. I didn't say I'd read them, and he never asked.

The filing cabinet had been his father's. It was dotted with old labels and American flag stickers. When it was finally empty, we put it out on the street.

I cooked pork chops in garlic and red wine and cleaned the kitchen while John took phone calls. He'd started a production company with a meek, diligent graduate student. It had begun as a lark, but John's childhood friends Felix and Victoria had somehow found money in Calgary, people who wanted to invest in a production company in New York with connections to Alberta. They called the company Cloudberry Productions. *I'm a real wife,* I thought, setting the table with cloth napkins. It felt like a parlor game.

John and Felix and Felix's wife, Victoria, had all grown up together, and John and Felix acted like brothers. They insulted each other constantly, but they did it while laughing. John didn't have any blood siblings. Neither did I.

After high school, they had all gone to college in Calgary, and after that, John had moved to New York, the only one in his whole class.

Victoria worked full-time as a legal secretary, and Felix was the primary parent to their three children. This made them strange. For their other high school friends, the women were always the wives.

John was still an artist, but now he was an entrepreneur, too. I practiced saying the word out loud so it sounded effortless, normal, not an aberration at all. *Entrepreneur.* The company would be easy to run, John had explained, and it would fund his art career. It was easy to be a writer—all I needed was time—but John needed to buy supplies and ship pieces and travel to shows and meet collectors. His career was more expensive and more difficult than mine, and the potential return was greater. Lucky for us, the production company would become profitable almost immediately. He showed me a spreadsheet that I didn't understand. He explained that we would soon be rich.

John would make a lot of money, and I'd still be a writer, alone with my thoughts. It would be like having two lives. Instead of adding hot water to a cupful of dehydrated chili, I'd eat sushi with John. The dream money swirled around us. I was an island of thrift within it, but it still touched me. The money felt like dress-up. It was a costume. I didn't need it, but it was good to have.

A waterfall of paper responsibilities flooded the house, books and manuscripts to address with polite enthusiasm while I gradually learned that John had never sent a thank-you note or deep-cleaned the house except for a party.

I needed him to share in the housekeeping, to have one date with me per week, to have two intimate sessions with me per week, to socialize with friends biweekly, and to pay me back the seven grand that he still owed me.

He'd started calling his photography installations *art that moves*. John said his phrase with a little hitch in his voice to suggest that he'd just thought of it that very moment, and also that he thought very highly of himself for thinking of it.

The night before John had to leave to install his first solo art show, the rotating platforms for his photographs were delivered. They were a half inch too short on each side. There was no way to fix them. It was a four-thousand-dollar mistake. We were sitting at the big blue table John had made out of police barriers, the table that would stand on our deck and fill with carpenter bees in a few years, after we moved to California and then back again.

I sat across from John and prepared to let the wave of shame wash over us. This was his first big show. I watched John to see what he would do. He sat and held his head in his hands, silent. No tears fell. I saw the shame pass by him like a specter.

He didn't mention it to the curators, and he didn't prepare for the lecture he had to give at the opening.

A week after he got home, the museum sent a note informing him that they were disappointed in his lecture and in the show. After that day he never spoke of it again.

The trouble with getting engaged is that the second you mention it to some people, they start screaming at you that if you haven't already registered for gifts and planned your honeymoon, you're mentally ill.

I asked John whether he was nervous about getting married and he just smiled and said, *No.*

I got drunk on white wine at a bar and dragged John home for a glorious session. Still feeling good, I scheduled a meeting with him to discuss our honeymoon. I asked him when he'd be able to buy the plane tickets with his credit card miles, and he got quiet. A sneer grew in his beautiful mouth.

Then he said, *I get to not talk about money if I don't want to,* and I said, *We aren't ready to get married.*

Walking on the beach during our honeymoon, we passed a gaggle of drunk women. One of them said, *Look at their rings, how bright they are! They're probably on their honeymoon!*

John had ordered himself a custom-made hammered white gold ring. I'd ordered the most basic yellow gold band I could find online. Over the years it got scratched up and dulled, and I loved taking it off and looking at how smooth it was on the inside, how it seemed to glow, how it was perfect.

When I was young, all that fathers ever had to do was sit in offices, eat at restaurants for lunch, do whatever they wanted wherever they went, and then come home and appear hardworking and loyal. Loyal, just for coming home to eat food and enjoy a clean and well-run house that a woman maintained just so a father could do whatever he wanted inside and outside of it.

I wrote to Hannah, *Tonight I learned why my mother always squealed and shrank away when my father tried to touch her: She was a fortress. And inside that fortress was rage, and in the center of that rage was the pain of the insult of being treated like a stupid maid. My fortress is the same, with smaller hips, surrounded by a corona of migraine.*

John said he would do the dishes and be in bed by eleven to fuck. At eleven o'clock, alone in the house, I did the dishes.

When he got home he explained why he was late. It didn't make sense. He taunted me, *You can't even follow a conversation,* and then, unable to stop the torrent of his confusing explanation, I yelled, *Quiet!* and then he shoved me and said, *Get out*.

After that, I cried from the deepest part of the pain tank, took a tranquilizer, and slept until noon.

When I finally got out of bed, we agreed to do our best to take care of each other and forgive each other.

Then John said that he wouldn't be able to put his share in the joint account that month, after all. I took a deep breath; at once my back seized up and I understood why people divorce.

I'd already asked John to email me his itinerary for Calgary, where he was going to meet with Felix's uncle, a venture capitalist. Vibrating like a tuning fork, I sent him the same email for the fourth time. When he finally responded, I explained, *Since I can't control my personal life, my professional life, and my financial life right now, when I also lose control of my social calendar, it feels like the last straw.*

John wrote back, *I'm really sorry, I thought I'd sent this to you. I love you very much.*

UPS lost track of yet another shipment of lights that John needed to finish his new film. He was on the phone for three days, impotent, filing complaints. I put on my boots and my warmest coat and went outside to look for the UPS truck. The snow was ankle-deep and made everything quiet.

In ten minutes I was back with the shipment, my arms wrapped around its slippery wet cardboard box.

At our scheduled household budget meeting, John spent half an hour recalculating the expenses I'd calculated. At one point, when he said he didn't have money to produce his art show and contribute to the household, I said, *So basically you're living in my house.*

But John and his co-founder had landed an investment in their little film production company, and we would move to Los Angeles to staff it and build it in a cheap warehouse space. I feared that, after we moved west, John would divide his time between Cloudberry and his art, and I would be a lonely wife with no support system, maybe saddled with a baby, unable to write or teach—a real wife, the one thing I'd sworn to myself I'd never be.

———

At an art dealer's party, John drank too much and spoke too carelessly and too long with the wrong people.

When I prompted him, he admitted he'd noticed that powerful people never get drunk at parties. Then he said, *I don't want to be a footnote in someone else's biography.*

I'd just sold another book. It was my biography that he was talking about.

John's mother sent a photo card of the four of us on the Brooklyn Bridge. *In June we welcomed John's wife, Jane, into our family. Happy Holidays.*

Every few weeks I remembered something I'd said to John within days of meeting him. *I'm kind of a workaholic,* I'd said. And immediately he'd said, *Oh, thank God.*

I'd found someone for whom making art was central and being in a relationship was incidental. I loved sitting in a room with John, both of us on our laptops, working silently, fiercely. I could feel our energies awake and together. We didn't need anything else from each other.

But by then I knew that John was often the one who arrived late to a party, overstayed his welcome, and forgot the gift. When I asked him if he'd be better off with a servant-wife than a human wife, he said, *I get up and shower and have breakfast waiting for me, and nine times out of ten you do the laundry and think about dinner and remind me to mail things and make phone calls . . . I can't imagine anyone being more helpful.*

He gave me a look of love. I felt wonderful. Then I felt trapped.

After John left to work in his studio, saying he'd grab a sandwich at the diner and be home by nine, I packed our things and hailed a cab and moved us from one sublet to another. We were bouncing around in those last days before our cross-country move.

As I unpacked, prepared to teach a class, and cooked myself dinner, I thought that maybe John would do something nice for me since I'd done so much for him in the past few weeks. At nine he called, drunk, having gone out with a friend, and asked me if I'd made dinner yet, and could he have some.

When he got home, he said he'd been stewing about some slightly belittling thing I'd said to him in front of someone else. He tossed his head like a teenager. What he failed to remember was that I'd said the slightly belittling thing mere moments after he'd stopped flirting with a messily drunk woman while I sat alone and ashamed with Hannah and her new boyfriend.

Agreeing to be someone's wife should be done only if you can't help yourself, I thought, but of course no one can help herself.

Then we moved to Los Angeles. I'd never driven on a freeway. The sun gave me migraines and also, somehow, one giant freckle in the middle of my forehead.

We bought a sofa and a car. John spent ten-hour days at Cloudberry, setting up the office, and I sat on the sofa in our otherwise empty house, staring into my laptop, waiting for our things to arrive. We slept on an air mattress. It was surprisingly cold at night.

I asked everyone I knew to connect me with people who wanted to work on their writing, one-on-one. That first year I had a dozen private students. Because of my preexisting autoimmune condition I couldn't get in-state health insurance, and this lack produced a fog of anxiety that followed me wherever I went.

One of my students came over for a one-on-one session and sat beside me while I went through my notes on her manuscript. After a few minutes John sat down across from us and started offering general advice on writing. I couldn't believe it, but my instinct was to pretend that nothing was happening, to protect the sheen of normalcy of the person who thought it would be appropriate to sit down and become my student's other teacher.

Was he demonstrating that he knew more than she did, or that he knew more than I did? Did he need her attention or mine? The reality I wanted didn't include this event, so I stepped around it and continued on.

A few weeks later a neighbor came over to borrow a screwdriver. I went to the kitchen, opened the cabinet under the sink, and took out my red toolbox while John ran to the garage to get one of his tools. Why lend someone two screwdrivers? The neighbor took both screwdrivers with a friendly smile. When she returned them later in the day, I asked her which screwdriver she'd used. John was lurking in the next room. I could hear him breathing. *I knew you'd ask that,* she sweetly said. *I used both of them equally.*

My father said that John had three things in his life—his production company, his art, and me—and that I couldn't be the third priority. He added, *You're smarter than I am,* but I wasn't even smart enough to remember not to get married.

I taught John how to open and sort all his mail: shred, trash, file, action items. I found a coupon for free document shredding. I dealt with the action items. All he needed to do from then on was sign checks and documents.

After I sent the final email to confirm the housewarming party I'd been planning for a month, John said, *Wait, I'm going to be in Calgary that night.*

I took one of John's favorite mugs out of the cupboard, shattered it on the front steps, carefully swept up all the pieces, and then cleaned the entire house.

My old friend Eben, who had been married longer than anyone I knew, said, *I can only recommend moving forward.* Eben and I had grown up together and had lately become close again. He was a life stage or two ahead of me, with a mortgage and a baby, and his insights were useful. By then he'd lived in Los Angeles for ten years.

I sobbed and stammered when I told John I'd been unhappy since we'd moved to California for his job, which required him to travel much of the time and might not last the year. I had neither the solace of company nor the solace of financial stability nor the solace of utility to others. I'd thought I was trading the last thing for the other two, but in reality I'd just been giving everything up.

And yet no married woman I knew was any better off, so I determined to carry on. After all, a person can be grandiose without being a clinical narcissist. And I was a control freak, a neat freak, a crazy person. A long time ago, in my twenties, I'd even spent ten days on a psych ward after a hospital-administered overdose of steroids for my autoimmune condition. John seemed awed by that hospitalization. He seemed to think it was cool, that I was a legitimately mad artist, touched with fire.

I decided to examine my rage, determine what I needed, and rely on John for no part of it. I imagined never needing to ask him for anything ever again.

By noon I'd showered, dressed, tidied the house of John's shoes and clothes, put away laundry, swept the floor, watered the garden, moved boxes to the garage, cooked breakfast, eaten, done the dishes, taken out the recycling, handled correspondence, and made the bed. John had gotten up and taken a shit.

For our first anniversary, the paper anniversary, I collected the hundreds of paper business cards he'd collected from people who might be interested in investing in Cloudberry, and added them to his online address book. John built me a pretty new website.

He said that since getting married he felt he'd lost a weight he didn't know he'd been carrying.

Then he told me that he'd sent a new collector the art piece she'd bought six months earlier and that it had arrived broken. Five minutes later I shitted a gallon.

Elegies are the best love stories because they're the whole story.

After we agreed to meet in the desert for Christmas, John's mother made a reservation for us at a ski mountain. Then she announced that we'd all drive up together and spend a week.

When John told her we'd spend two nights, as discussed, she called him and said, *I sure would love it if you could spend more time with us.*

She withheld all information about the place, hoping we'd just give up asking.

Disclosing only five days beforehand the no-pets rule, John's mother said she'd pay for us to board our cat.

She told us each this news separately.

At the end of my email she added, *I feel bad!*

Her cancer was in remission, but she knew that John was still afraid she'd die.

For Christmas we gave her herbal tea, almonds, and artisanal cooking salt.

She left the gifts on the kitchen counter and ate blocks of grocery-store cheese, cookies, cake, and cinnamon rolls spread with half an inch of butter.

Every afternoon John's stepfather drove their rented Jeep five hundred yards into town and bought a few more things.

Christmas dinner was at a restaurant draped in polyester napkins, all the food sprinkled with powdered cheese, chocolate syrup drizzled on the dessert plates.

An old friend emailed some photos of her baby. There should be a word for the feeling that comes when your most neurotic friends bear children before you do. Surprise. Confusion. Shame.

That night John said, *I have a lot of guilt about how unsettled our lives have been since we moved here.* I said, *I didn't know that.* And at that moment, the veil lifted.

Then he got weeping drunk. *I'm so proud of you,* he kept saying. *I know that there are hard things, but there are also glamorous things,* he said, referring to being with me, being broke, getting to go to the Akadimía. *I don't have any cushion and my credit cards are maxed out. I don't know what I'm going to do . . .*

After investing five years of my life, I didn't want to have to start over again.

Then he said, *I know how disappointed you are,* and I poured tears.

I had two friends whose lives seemed palatable, who had jobs befitting their intelligence and education. Both of their husbands were dying of impotent rage.

I'd given up two and a half years of my academic career for Cloudberry, following John around in lieu of going on the market for a full-time teaching job. I was a layer cake of abandonment and hurt and fury, iced with a smile.

I thought, *If I had the energy I'd leave him,* and then I folded up that little thought, wrapped it in gauze, and swallowed it.

After Cloudberry landed its first big project, John's co-founder wanted to reallocate everyone's equity.

When John refused to hand over his equity to an outside financial advisor, the advisor told John he was fired. He didn't have the power to do that, but then John's partner stopped picking up the phone.

John started calling everyone at the company who still took his calls. I took a tranquilizer with lunch and began writing a call log, not knowing what else to do.

When the tranquilizer wore off I started shaking. John marched me into the bedroom and lay me down, supine. He lay on top of me, his heavy body weighing me down from shoulders to ankles. The pressure calmed me. It always did.

There were holes in my days then, through which I dropped out of the bottom of my life and found myself inconsolable by anything in the known world. I visualized hanging myself from the lemon tree.

John's next day job would drag us either across town or across the country, back to New York. The circumstances of my life were no longer mine to control.

Then Eve's cancer came back.

I wrote to her, *When I first met John and saw that he admired strong women, I knew he must have a strong mother. Thank you for the love you gave him, and for raising him to be a funny and gentle person. I know you must be so proud of him. I'm so glad I found him.*

Then I heard John on the phone, telling his mother, *I might have to move back to New York for these jobs* instead of using the first-person-plural pronoun. My skin started to fizz with shame. He was the main character, and I was his wife. His mother had also been a wife. Wives and more wives, all the way down.

While I deep-cleaned the kitchen, John scrubbed the tub and vacuumed. Watching him clean made me want to get pregnant. But being pregnant and materially dependent on my husband felt dangerous. Even using the word *husband* felt unsafe.

Later in the day he said, *I love you so much. Every time I read your work I fall in love with you again.*

I'd never wanted a child, and John and I had both always been artists first, adamantly, with no urge to marry or procreate. Lately John seemed to think we could have a child, but I didn't think two artists could raise a child, that there must be a wife somewhere, but I didn't want to be a wife, but if I were a wife, I knew I'd be very good at it.

I enjoyed meeting my husband's old friends when they came through town, people to whom I was known only as Mrs. Bridges, even though I hadn't changed my name to John's. I was in drag as his wife, and no one knew. They thought I was complicit.

When I was twenty weeks pregnant, John got a job back in New York, at a bank. The money was good. John was concerned that working full-time at a bank, even as a creative director, would depress him, but he thought it was still the best thing to do. He would support our little family once the baby came.

Eve's cancer had stopped responding to chemotherapy. John spoke to her so tenderly. It was his voice, but it was also the voice of a heartbroken child.

Over the next week John would fly to New York, find us an apartment, and then fly to Alberta to see his mother.

The night before he left, John said that he might not find an apartment in the three days he'd budgeted, that we might have to crash on a couch for a while.

—So stay until you find an apartment and get to Alberta two days later.

—Instead of spending time with my dying mom?

He refused to discuss it further.

He got an apartment in New York, and I met him in Alberta. By then I could feel the baby kicking, but no one else could feel it through the outside of me yet.

I stood in front of Eve for a long time while she held her hands on my belly and pressed her ear to it, as if to listen.

She was very thin but still able to walk a slow mile. I walked with her, and then we both took naps.

One night she needed oxygen. John's stepfather led her into the bedroom. A few minutes later, he came out and said that she was feeling better and wanted to speak with me.

I went inside. It was just the two of us. I didn't know that this was the last time I'd ever see her. I didn't know that this was her deathbed confession.

She told me that when she was in college, after she'd told her parents she was marrying her first husband, John's father, her parents had offered her a yearlong trip to Europe if she didn't marry him.

They'd hoped she'd have some Continental romance and forget about the guy.

After she said that, she put a blue fentanyl lollipop into her mouth and closed her eyes.

On the ride back to our hotel I told John what his mother had said. She'd never told him that story, and neither of us understood why she'd told it to me then.

That night I dreamt of waking up in a hospital bed and finding I'd given birth in my sleep. A tiny, perfect boy was seated at the foot of my bed, waiting for me to be his mother. He was sweet and easy to nurse.

While I was on the phone about John's lost luggage and tax lien, he ordered a single-sized futon to be delivered to our new New York apartment for us to sleep on. I'd have told him he was an idiot, but he knew.

———

In yet another bureaucratic emergency, we learned that our credit would be destroyed unless we obtained signed documents from John's former business partner, who no longer answered the phone when John called. I persuaded the state government to skip a step and fix the administrative error for the third-party company that had made it.

My anxieties were whirling around like a carousel in front of my face, so I drank a glass of warm milk and fell dead asleep for two hours.

Right after I awoke, my shoulders seized up, and John agreed to massage them. I pressed down on a painful knot. *Here.*

John rubbed all around the knot. He said, *Everything is connected. These muscles are all part of a system.* He rubbed my shoulder blade, getting farther and farther away from the pain. I dug my finger into the lump, trying to soften it.

Stop it, John said. *I know what I'm doing.* He didn't touch the sore spot.

He would decide whether I deserved relief. He would decide whether my pain even existed at all.

I wrote to Eve, *Things aren't great right now.* She wrote back, *You're going through so much carrying the babe, and working, and being hit off and on with fatigue and pregnancy brain, and your London trip approaching.*

My most recent book had been nominated for a prize, and the five nominees were invited to a ceremony in London. It would be our last trip before the baby came.

Two days before the trip, John went out late and I fell asleep, my body weary from fetal assembly.

The doorbell rang at three in the morning. A stranger's voice sounded on the intercom: *Does John Bridges live here?* I ran downstairs in my pajamas, my pregnant belly bulging over the waistband.

A stranger had brought my bloody, vomiting, concussed husband home. He couldn't open his eyes, respond to questions, or finish a sentence.

The stranger said he'd found John splayed on the sidewalk, face down.

We'd just moved to that apartment a month ago. My first thought was, *I have to clean up this vomit or we'll be evicted.* I ran upstairs and got some towels and waddled back downstairs and mopped up the vomit on my hands and knees. John gurgled. He was leaning against the wall. His head drooped. A viscous strand hung from his mouth. He was trying to say something. He was trying to say, *You're welcome.*

I called 911. The EMTs arrived. The stranger handed off my husband to them. The EMTs snuck looks at my enormous belly and smelled the tequila vomit and looked into my eyes, silently telling me I was an idiot for having a child with this man.

They wheeled John out. I rode in the back of the van. I had his insurance card and ID. I knew his Social Security number by heart.

They wheeled John into a curtained nook in Emergency. John kept trying to get up from the stretcher to go to the bathroom, but he wasn't allowed. I couldn't keep him from getting up. I asked a nurse for a urinal, which John refused to use. I asked for a clean sheet, which I spread on the floor. I lay down on it and tried to sleep. I wondered what the fetus was doing.

The emergency department diagnosed acute alcohol intoxication, a possible concussion, and a shattered nose. No brain bleed was found on the CAT scan, but I'd have to monitor him for forty-eight hours for signs of a slow bleed.

I called my literary agent and told him where I was.

We didn't go to London.

The next day I flashed back to the image of John meekly standing in the entryway, his head bowed, vomiting and drooling and bleeding. I'd have those flashbacks for years, every time John was late to meet me anywhere.

I canceled and postponed and scheduled things. Food, water, shower, clean clothes.

I said to my mother, *I might never be the same.* She said, *You will.*

It's never happened before. It won't happen again, John said, once he sobered up.

He'd had two beers with a small lunch, and then, at the bar, eaten a few bites of food and steadily drunk tequila. He remembered looking at his watch at two o'clock in the morning. Getting into an unlicensed cab and then getting out when the guy said he needed to fill the gas tank. Hailing a real cab, feeling unsteady on his feet. He remembered riding in the cab over the bridge. He might have passed out in the cab, and then again when he got out, but once he got up off the ground he was able to tell a stranger his full name and address.

I walked to the corner and found a sticky pool of blood on the sidewalk.

I did laundry, bagged trash, dealt with mail, fed and played with the cat, cooked, iced John's nose, bandaged his fingers, fed him meals and vitamins and Gatorade and water, did dishes, calculated our October expenses, answered emails from my publishers, bought groceries, went to the drugstore, cleaned the bathroom, made the bed, did calisthenics, and so on. I just went from task to task, slowly, so I didn't have to think about anything.

Hannah told me to buy a life insurance policy.

Months later, the baby wailing in its crib, I sat in the bathroom past eleven at night, shaking and sobbing, calling John over and over and over, certain that he'd fallen in the street again. When he finally got home he said his phone had died while he was playing a video game.

I sent a gift card to the guy who'd brought John home.

You saved John's life. I can never thank you enough.

His blood alcohol level was above 0.3 percent and he had a concussion. By some miracle the CAT scan didn't show a brain bleed, but he's being monitored for forty-eight hours in case there's a slow one going.

If he'd been left in the street he'd very likely have choked to death.

I was freaking out when I saw him because he'd never been drunk like that before. In all the years I've known him he's never passed out, never blacked out, never even vomited. Apparently his co-workers—he just started at a new job—were doing tequila shots. On empty stomachs. John left the bar first. God knows what happened to them.

That you selflessly decided to let yourself be vomited and bled on by a complete stranger (NB: John has no communicable diseases, so no need to get checked for hepatitis or anything) is the reason our son, when he's born in January, will have a father.

If you ever feel, ever in your life, that you haven't done enough, or haven't lived up to your potential—whatever form that takes for you—please remember what you did for my family. Your help absolutely saved us. I hope I can do as much in my life as you did on Thursday.

I slept a little better that night but was still haunted by the image of John standing in the entryway with his head lolling forward, froth hanging.

My mother said, *Boys will be boys*. John's mother thought my biggest regret was that John had ruined my London trip.

Soon after that, John and I agreed that he couldn't say I wasn't supporting him while his mother died and I couldn't say he wasn't supporting me during my pregnancy. It felt like progress. At least we were even.

While he had two nasal fractures reset, I sat in the hospital waiting room for six hours, aching from Braxton-Hicks contractions and watching my phone die.

That night John said to me, *I know I haven't been the perfect husband . . .*

The next day I fell on the sidewalk while doing errands but managed to land on my hands and knees.

Eve hadn't been able to keep food down for a couple of weeks. She didn't want to stop chemo, but she said she understood that she wasn't going to get better.

When she checked herself into the hospital through Emergency, her weight was down to ninety-eight pounds.

Then John went away alone for a week to an art show in Miami, for parties and drinks, and I sat in the apartment, remembering why we hadn't gone to London, and what I'd had to do instead.

My psychiatrist said it would be all right to ask John to come home because I needed him. John agreed to look at plane tickets.

Hannah said, *You can't be the only one who cares enough to call off a trip to take care of someone when they're incapacitated.*

John asked me to call the hotel in Miami and get him a refund. It was my own fault for having been his free concierge service for so long. For having been his wife. I refused.

Then he flew home. When he saw that Hannah was there, taking care of me, he was resentful.

I thought I was rescuing you. I wanted to stay one more day.

Then I erupted into screaming sobs.

I wrote to my mother, *Today John's office had a party to celebrate a successful pitch, and John hasn't finished the video for it, but he had to leave the office for my doctor's appointment since he'd missed the last two appointments, but he missed this appointment, too, because his cab was stuck in traffic, and now there's a shipment coming to his studio in Brooklyn, and he needs to leave work again to meet it this afternoon, since there's only one set of keys and he has it. I expect him to get fired by spring. No one can live the way he's been living. That, and there's a chance I'll give birth while he's in Alberta visiting his dying mother over Christmas.*

I feared that John would lose his job and our insurance, and that I'd have to divorce him to escape his debts, and that he'd die, and that I'd lose my mind and be committed somewhere, and my parents would have to file for bankruptcy and put our baby in an orphanage. I wanted to be at least five steps away from that last terrible event.

The five-hour birthing class was the most intimate physical contact John and I had had in months, and I loved it. Then we got home and John declared that we needed to get a new apartment immediately, that he didn't like the layout of ours, and I had a screaming, sobbing meltdown and then cried torrentially for two hours.

Then he was gone again, lost in work, planning a new series of photographic sculptures. I was too tired to care.

While John was uptown at the bank, I waited in his art studio for five hours for a FedEx truck that he'd sent to the wrong address and that never arrived. There was no heat in the studio. I was exhausted and heavily pregnant. I drowsed on the sofa in my winter coat, getting up every thirty minutes to piss in the sink. The fetus had compressed my bladder. Each time I pissed I had to do it in front of a wall of windows, on the other side of which was a working industrial plant.

The obstetrician on call declared my likelihood of delivering in the next four days small but not zero. John's mother was in hospice. He wanted to fly to Alberta. *You have to decide who needs you more,* John's best friend told him. John's stepfather left a desperate voicemail saying that Eve wanted John to stay with me. *If you really want me to stay I'll stay,* John said to me. *I really want you to stay,* I said.

My cervix was starting to ripen and I had a cold, which put me in the autoimmune disease relapse zone. John said, *What do we do if you have a relapse?* before I mentioned it.

Three thousand miles away, a nurse held her phone to the dying woman's ear. *Hi, Mom,* John said, and I felt it in the middle of my body.

The next day the nurse called to say that Eve had reached out for her husband and said, *I love you.* Then she'd tried to pull out her tubes, and her morphine was increased until she lay still.

The next night, she died.

John said he had to go to the ocean, so I booked an apartment on Long Island for the weekend.

Here's the story again, smaller:

On the day Eve died, we got up at six in the morning to go to the hospital. I had a sonogram and we learned that the fetus was almost seven pounds and had a healthy heart. John went to work and I went home. I made a turkey meatloaf. We ate in bed. I got John's phone turned back on. He'd forgotten to pay the bill. I made cocoa. Then his stepfather called.

We drove along the beach, ate bar food, and watched television on our last trip before the baby was born. We were happy, laughing.

When we got home, we found that an inch of the upstairs neighbors' bathwater had dripped through a crack in the ceiling into the bathroom. Minutes after I cleaned it up, the ceiling fell in. Reinforced concrete, drywall, wood, brick, dust everywhere.

We opened the windows to let in some fresh air. When we got into bed, the cat was looking in through the glass terrace door, having gone out into the snow at some point.

Eve had only ever worn costume baubles, but my mother was in a frenzy.

—*Did John get his mother's jewelry?*

—*Why, do you want it?*

—*No. But before her husband gives it to other women.*

—*Eve didn't have a lot of jewelry.*

—*Well, not just jewelry. He's going to try to take it.*

—*I don't know where you get these ideas.*

—*This is the real world, you know.*

She was trying to tell me that passing down jewelry to daughters and daughters-in-law is one of the few small ways that women retain power in a system designed to keep them helpless.

My mother was the only person I knew who hadn't been hoodwinked into thinking that those days were long over, but back then I was sure that she was crazy.

My parents came to meet the baby. My mother was holding an obviously secondhand oversized teddy bear with a rumpled $50 price tag on it. My father hugged me. My mother didn't seem to know how to hold the infant and didn't think to wash her hands until I told her to. She said that a stranger had stayed in my parents' house until I was four weeks old, taking care of me day and night. I hadn't known that.

My parents sat in the apartment watching me change diapers and feed and soothe the baby. When I suggested they could run to the laundromat, my mother said, *We can drop off the stuff and you can pick it up later*. I said, *That isn't actually helpful*.

I tried to explain that nursing is complicated, and that I never seemed to be able to calculate when to pump and when to nurse and when to sleep and when to let the child sleep, and how to manage engorgement and nipple pain. John rolled his eyes, and I said, *One of the last things your mother told you was to be nicer to me*.

I got up and went to the kitchen for a glass of iced tea. John called to me, *It's considered polite, when getting yourself a glass of tea, to offer the other person a glass of tea*. I walked back to him and said, *Instead of saying that to your exhausted wife, you should be thanking me for all the things I do for you, the baby, this family, and this house every day that you take absolutely for granted*. And then he apologized. He truly apologized.

Later in the day he called me from work, still feeling sorry.

If I removed the baby from my lap he screamed, so I sat all day, my back seizing, my thumb in his mouth, the white noise machine spreading its headache over the apartment, the cat crying, wondering how I thought I'd be able to write a book review and plan a fall-semester poetry course.

John kept reminding me to record everything, not understanding that a sleep-deprived person doesn't notice what to record.

At the end of some argument he said, *Fuck you*, and closed the bedroom door behind him. Walking away—his ace in the hole when he knew he was wrong. I can't even remember what day that was.

The baby lay under his toy arch, wiggling and smiling at the hanging beads. I watched him in his private happiness.

John said that he had nothing to give me because he knew his life was harder than mine. I poured tears for a whole hour. He told me I was acting like a spoiled child, that the postpartum period was so much easier than his life, working at the bank instead of being an artist. He refused to take antidepressants, claiming it would take too long to find the proper dose. I wanted neither a divorce nor a disdainful partner, so there I was, hoping for a third option.

Hannah and her second husband had had a baby two years earlier. She said that her husband had also failed to recognize the invisible work of nursing and caring for their child, and that they'd had the same arguments about whose life was harder and why Hannah wasn't getting any work done.

To solve the problem, she said, *I became a lot more patient.*

John got home from work on a Saturday too depressed to care properly for the baby, sulking because he hated his job and because he couldn't spend all night in the studio before we all flew to Alberta in the morning for his mother's funeral.

Meanwhile I looked in three stores for infant sunscreen, got the laundry done, packed and planned and cleaned the house and nursed the baby seven times and changed him and played with him and took him outside in the carrier when he wouldn't stop crying. No one paid any attention to the cat crying at the suitcases.

John had three double gin and tonics on the plane and got messy, which made me cry. The baby was terrifically sweet.

By the time we got back to New York, John had fixated on the idea that moving back to California was the only thing that would ever make him feel better. He said that my choosing to remain in New York and finish teaching my poetry course equaled choosing to keep him depressed. *It's your fault I'm depressed!* he said.

Then he went out for lumber and soil and brought home four chairs and made a picnic table and two planters.

You always want to make out after I make home improvements, he observed.

The baby fell asleep in the sling and slumped so far forward that a woman glared at me. When he faced front it was impossible to keep his sun hat from falling over his eyes, even when he wore it backward. He looked blindfolded and dead.

I walked home holding him upright with both hands, my left arm tingling.

The world didn't need me. Only the baby needed me.

One more hour. Less than an hour. Ten minutes. John returned.

On the first Mother's Day I spent as a mother, John was in a daze. Flowers? A card? As far as he was concerned, the only mother in the world was his, and she was dead.

We'd fallen into a groove: John made art on the weekends because he felt entitled to, and I did errands and chores on the weekends because I felt responsible.

The woman who cut my hair had spent ten years as an inpatient psychiatric nurse. Most of her patients had been exhausted women, she said, with drunk, useless husbands and too many children. Under lockdown, the women were on vacation, sleeping through the night and being brought meals on a tray.

At a party, while answering my question about her own marital troubles, a woman cut herself off by saying, *But you've been through so much.* Suddenly she needed me to have suffered more.

A few months later, John started another company. He'd somehow done it from within the bank, which had agreed to provide the initial funding. This company had ten times the venture capital of the first company, so it was ten times safer, he said. He'd come up with the idea of an internet-connected mirror. You could learn a new language while brushing your teeth. If you wanted to, you could practice the language while the mirror took video of you. Speech coaches would then evaluate your progress and send back custom-made lessons to help you learn faster. He called the company Polyglot.

We'd have to move back to Los Angeles. Office space and assistants were cheaper there than in New York.

John waltzed out the door to a three-hour drawing class while I cleaned the house, went to the laundromat, browsed used furniture online, and made chili. He came back—he'd wanted to draw a woman, and the model had been a man, so he sulked and played video games until his three hours were up.

I felt the usual fury, blanketed by the usual somnolence. I sat alone on the roof-deck, in the dark, cooling off after a hot bath. The big tree swayed. The Big Dipper blinked. The hundred-and-fifty-year-old building creaked. I was a small animal passing through on my way back into the earth.

We finally managed a penetrative session. The scar tissue from my episiotomy was lumpy but seemed to soften a little.

We celebrated John's birthday at a biergarten. He'd told half the guests to meet at a different bar, so they'd waited for an hour at the first spot. After three beers, he showed his friends how to pick up the baby. He lifted the baby up and down like a weight lifter.

He'd promised to vacuum the living room after the party, but by the end of the day he had back spasms from picking up the baby improperly. We ordered forty dollars' worth of sushi for dinner while I stewed about his tax debt. Then I cleaned the apartment.

After I finished the bedroom, where he was watching an action movie for the fiftieth time, he said to me, *I'm sorry I only cause you stress.*

A few hours later he asked me if I'd move to New Zealand if he got a job there, as if to neutralize the apology, or as if to punish me for having made him apologize.

The next day I dropped and bent the lid to the coffeepot. John scolded me and said we couldn't afford to replace everything I broke, and then we fought. That morning he'd bought yet another stack of comic books and overspent on fancy cheese, as he did every time we had guests.

That night John's friend Felix came over for dinner. Victoria had stayed in Calgary with the children.

Felix asked me how I was doing, and I said that I was having a hard time trying to teach and write since I'd had the baby. I had fifteen hours a week of babysitting. That was what we could afford; we paid for it with money from a fellowship that had come just in time.

Felix calmly said that raising kids is a full-time job, and why was I even trying to write or teach. His children, a son and twin daughters, were older than my child. He was so certain, so serene. I envied him.

All the mothers I knew were in awe of how little we were able to do, after all our education, after having been told that we'd be able to do anything, after having children in America. We'd all assumed we'd continue our lives as before, and that the only difference would be a child or children silently napping in bassinets or playing with toys while we worked. We hadn't known we'd be holding grimly on to screaming, incontinent, vomitous creatures twenty hours a day. Breastfeeding made me very thirsty, as people had said it would, and it made me crave cigarettes even though I'd never liked the taste of them.

At the playground with their babies, all the neurotic mothers confided in John. When I mentioned it afterward, he said, *Animals and children, too. It's because I'm calm.*

The next morning I woke up screaming, *Help, help,* from a nightmare in which my parents watched me die and did nothing to help me. Upon waking I thought, *This is great! I'm really accessing some deep, old material.*

When John got up he said he'd be spending that weekend in the studio, and maybe that night, too. I had a screaming meltdown and said, *You disgust me*. Then John took the train to work. An hour later he emailed me and said he had diarrhea.

The trouble with spending the day with a small child is that at the end of it you're physically exhausted, mentally emptied, and you have nothing to show for it but a filthy house, filthy clothes, raw and peeling hands, and the inability to see beyond babyhood.

My personality and life had been swallowed by motherhood, and every few days, my husband threw the fact that I didn't have a full-time job in my face. The work of caring for the baby was invisible to him.

The child tantrummed until he choked himself quiet, but a couple of days before that, he'd tried to pick up a freckle from my arm.

Why are you so angry? My husband frequently asked me why I was so much angrier than other women. It always made me smile. I was exactly as angry as every other woman I knew.

It wasn't that we'd been born angry; we'd become women and ended up angry.

Anger is one of the last privileges of the truly helpless. Infants are angry. Have you ever sat all night holding a baby in the dark who's screaming right into your face? It changes you, or so my husband used to say. He'd done that one night, sat and been screamed at. I was sitting right next to him, but he always told the story as if he'd been the only one there. All the other days and nights, it had just been me. But that one night had been the real game-changer, apparently.

My mother told me I'd been such a happy child. *You loved everything,* she said. I became angry early, though. I was precocious.

I pitied men for having to stay the same all their lives, for missing out on this consuming rage.

We got a sitter and went out to dinner. John picked the restaurant. The entrées were horrifically expensive, the amount of an entire dinner bill.

John encouraged me to order a first course and then an entrée. He ordered an entire bottle of wine. Already in for a pound, we ordered dessert, too, and coffee. The bill came to more than four hundred dollars.

I felt cold. My body tingled. I wanted to vomit.

This is an experience! John said. *This is what we should be spending money on, experiences!*

But it wasn't an experience. It was food, and we'd turn it into shit, no different from the shit we'd make of whatever else we ate.

At home I never relaxed; the child always required attention. I crouched, waiting to feed him or help sharpen a crayon or brush his teeth. That wariness prevented deep immersion in anything else. I couldn't write, couldn't even think, for in order to think or write I needed time to fight my natural buoyancy and swim effortfully down to the bottom of the sea, where no light is, where I could live in my mind's eye, and where nothing mattered except the thought.

When I'd had jury duty I'd achieved a sort of euphoria. My phone had died a few hours in, and I'd brought a book. I read until I couldn't read anymore. I sat and relaxed and waited, alone with my thoughts or chatting with the other serenely bored people.

At home I was bored, too, but innumerable short sessions of boredom throughout the day damaged the spirit more than being bored for seven hours at a stretch.

With the child, I was always ready to be interrupted. I couldn't swim to the bottom; I couldn't hear him down there. So I stayed on the surface, doing crossword puzzles, which required full attention and mimicked the sort of mental state I enjoyed on the sea floor. It mimicked that state, but even if I finished a puzzle, the result was worthless. There was no residue, nothing that lasted.

It was like housework, which consists of tasks that, by design, get undone every day. Every day there are dishes and laundry. Sweep the kitchen floor, take out the garbage. Every day get the mail and sort it. Every day read and answer email. Every day wash the body. The bathroom gets dirty; clean it. Vacuum and wipe the floors and the furniture. Clothing gets outgrown and tattered; barbers and dentists and doctors must be visited. No time for deep attention, just a thousand tasks.

I'd initially started doing more of the housework because I was at home more, because I earned less, and the housework became a sort of penance, or a way to prove my value. Soon I was doing everything, and John accused me of trying to control everything, but his accusation, though correct, failed to acknowledge the reason it was happening.

I felt bereft before John's business trip to Calgary. His main investors lived there, and so did half the board. Alberta connections are tight. I cleaned the house like a madwoman as if to scrub away all trace of him, to make a tidy place in which to feel lonely.

The child walked confidently all over the apartment, all day long. Occasionally he rested against a wall and cried, as if grieving for the days when Mama carried him.

Then one day he ate half of a banana all by himself. And though he hadn't eaten the pasta I'd made the week before, I made some more for supper and he ate three bowls. I fed him with a spoon. By the end he was grinning and clapping his hands between bites.

After dinner he watched me use a wet rag to mop up some spilled milk. After I put down the rag, he picked it up and scrubbed just as he'd seen Mama do it.

Unable to focus on a book, I skimmed thousands of words online, trying not to give in to doing a crossword puzzle. Then in the afternoon the child couldn't stop coughing and started crying hysterically, refused to be held. I grabbed him and ran braless with him to the doctor in my dirty pajamas. By the time we arrived he'd coughed up the phlegm and stopped crying.

Then John came home from Calgary. The child cried when his father picked him up. I felt numb.

Spontaneous tiny hugs and tiny tantrums. The child had become a toddler, with big feelings. His pure, sobbing frustration was so beautiful.

The child scribbled with a crayon while John sneaked into the kitchen and ate the food I'd made the child for lunch.

That night, after teaching my class, I went out with the head of the department and rode the train home drunk. At Penn Station there was a jazz trio, three guys blasting sax, bass, and horn, and I tried to resist the urge to empty my wallet into their instrument case.

I looked the famous author up and down before I caught myself. God fucking damn it. I managed to sit with other colleagues at dinner. When it was time for my train, I made my way slowly around the long table. The famous author said he was sorry we hadn't gotten to gossip. *But we got a lot of that done last time,* he added.

Then, on the train home, something quite remarkable happened. Just sitting on the seat, vibrating with the train car hurling itself down the track, I came.

I took a long walk and ate lunch with my husband before he went to Calgary again for the weekend. To save money, he'd been staying with Felix and Victoria on his trips up north to see the Polyglot investors.

I always slept beautifully when he was away and began to suspect that he'd been waking me up at night.

I didn't know you would be here, the famous author said when I arrived at the book party. Before he left he put his arm around me for a moment, and I ran my hand down his back like an idiot.

Did you get your Porsche? I asked disdainfully, to punish him for my unmanageable feeling. He'd just received an enormous book advance and wanted to buy himself a vintage 911.

Strong, vibrating shame. I wanted to hit him with a car. I wanted to sit next to him at a dinner that would never happen, his fingers tickling the skin under my knee.

I wrote him the next morning at 7:42 A.M. with clear purpose. *I'm sorry I teased you about your Porsche. Please don't hate me.*

Then all I had to do was accept the fact that he wouldn't write back, and then discreetly masturbate about it for ten years.

But three hours later he wrote back. *I didn't realize you were teasing me until now, so just starting hating you this very minute. Plus, I may get a Jaguar instead and you will want a ride at some point.*

Two hours later, I wrote, *I'll try to stay on my best behavior.*

That afternoon I had to rub one out in my office before the faculty meeting.

The child hugged his soft little polar bear cub. Then he put it back in the toy box. Then he took it out again and hugged it again.

While I watched him I imagined a scandalously expensive lunch with the famous author, after which he suggested getting in a cab and going to a hotel.

I couldn't sleep for desire. Panting in bed next to my sleeping husband I worried I'd wake him. I wasn't even doing anything.

I pictured riding in a Jaguar with cream-colored leather.

That level of arousal couldn't possibly last.

I read the first few pages of the famous author's latest novel. The prose was bad, but seeing his name on the spine of the dust jacket, just lying there on the floor next to the bed, made me blush.

Weaning the child had caused me to ovulate for the first time in two years. That little egg was powerful.

John watched me prepare food, clean, and keep house all morning, then said, *Just so you know, I was planning on getting a massage during naptime today.*

In lieu of crying, I explained that instead of getting a massage he would buy gas for the grill and load the playpen and infant car seat into the car to bring back to Hannah.

When I spent time with women who didn't have children and explained that I hadn't worked much since having a baby and moving twice (soon thrice) across the country for John's jobs, they looked terrified by pity.

I froze the forty dollars' worth of scallops John had bought on a whim. When he called from work, I told him how unhappy I was and realized it was the longest he'd listened to me in a long time. If he'd been home he'd have talked over me, called me crazy, and walked out of the room.

That weekend we both got massages, one at a time, while the other stayed with the child. I felt the masseuse harvesting all the pain in my body. I was as pliant and unresistant as a blade of grass. I no longer cared what happened to me. I was ready for the pain. It was black, a layer of invisible black liquid inside my body. It all came out. The extraction was painful, like lancing a boil.

The massage triggered a massive shit, the silencing of my anxiety, a heavy sleep, and a feeling of intense well-being that led to calm, confident work on a book review.

The next day, John spent the whole day at home. I ran the house while he watched the child, and we traded off and each got a bit of work done. At the end of the day I said with perfect candor, *This is the best day I've had in a long time. Do you know why? Because I spent it with you.* I didn't even know I was going to say it until I said it.

That year I'd sworn we'd combine our money and get a financial counselor, but it was summer and we still hadn't done it. I felt foul shame about John's reckless spending.

Tantrums all day, sunburn and blisters and exhaustion.

When the child saw me dragging the big green laundry bag down the hall, he ran back to me and helped me drag it. After we got it inside, I told him he was a good helper, and he said, *Help*.

The child pushed the following items around in his toy stroller: a toy truck, a toy hammer, a book about trucks. He wasn't interested in pushing around the bunny.

John caught a cold and was too sick to celebrate our anniversary. Still, four years.

My love for the child had become incapacitating. It was hard not to go into his room and watch him sleep.

I had infinite patience with my one-year-old, whom I held to the behavioral standards of a two-year-old, and almost no patience with my husband, whom I held to the behavioral standards of a mother.

When John and I got home from an early dinner out, the babysitter said that the child had walked her to bath time and then to story time, and that she'd never seen a baby do that. *He's one in a million,* she said. *Some people thought I was crazy to keep him on such a tight schedule,* I said. She said, *You were NOT crazy.*

The next morning, John flew to Calgary for yet another meeting with the investors.

Before he left, he told me that I kept too strict a routine, for myself and for the child.

Overhearing me singing "Frog Went A-Courtin'" to the child, John said, *I feel so lucky that I have a wife with such a beautiful voice.*

John worked hard to support us. I'd just sold another book. I felt embarrassed by my luck.

I ovulated hard, as I always did then. I ovulated like a mother. Every time John was kind to me, my body immediately responded. It wanted me to get pregnant again, but we didn't have time to fuck before John flew back to Calgary.

I was exhausted by John's return—the mess, the dirt, the intolerably slow rate of completing tasks, the constant assumption that I wanted to watch videos on the internet. The child was still teething, crying, not sleeping. Some people still thought I had time to do anything but care for the child, run the house, maintain my marriage, and do the bare minimum of work necessary to convince myself I was still a writer.

I had a young child, twenty-five hours of child care per week, and a husband who worked hard and traveled constantly. I didn't go out. I didn't travel. I didn't exercise. I area-cleaned the house and thought in full sentences only when I slept.

One day my internal monologue suddenly became a strange voice telling me that John and the child would be better off without me, that I should just die, that I was worthless. *Feelings of worthlessness and suicidal ideation are symptoms of depression,* I told myself in the midst of it, but I felt as if someone was yelling those things at me all day.

The cat yowled in the night for two hours and I went mad with rage until John came home at one-thirty in the morning.

I felt overwhelmed by the prospect of moving across the country for the third time in less than four years. If we hadn't had John's art studio or a toddler or a cat, if we'd had child care and a house and cars waiting for us, if I weren't afraid of the freeway, if I weren't depressed, if—but even then it would still have been hard.

I took half a tranquilizer in the afternoon, worried about landing in California and John going to work twelve hours later and having no child care, no car, no internet, no ability to shower or buy food or interview babysitters.

John left for Calgary for another week. I took a tranquilizer after lunch, worrying the child would feel unsafe after we moved. The internet indicated that toddlers adjust easily. By evening I was almost convinced.

The cat meowed in the night while the child coughed.

John came home from Calgary but spent the afternoon packing up his art studio.

My hours were only ever fever-pitched or absolutely empty.

Then we moved back to Los Angeles. The flight was exactly as bad as I'd feared it would be—the child screamed and thrashed during the entire descent and for about half an hour midflight—but no worse.

John left for Calgary again. A babysitter came and showed me that I'd installed the car seat incorrectly. The movers arrived with our things before I could go out for soft food to pill the cat. The cat hid. The movers left. I unpacked a few things. I didn't have the energy anymore to blaze through it.

I set up some more sitter interviews. In one week we'd have child care and all our belongings and, dare to dream, curtains.

I know you can do it because you do it at night. I know you can do it because I know you're brave. I said this a thousand times in a row to get the child to stand calmly in his crib, then sit calmly down. Then I needed to change his diaper, and the spell was broken and I hardened my heart. Two hours later I went in and he was smiling, having fun all by himself.

Nothing but mothering and housewifery. I felt as if I'd let my car drift slowly off the road and into a snowbank. The airbag popped out. In big pink letters it said, *Congratulations! You're forty years old and completely financially dependent on your husband!*

During the worst fight of our marriage, I screamed, *Fuck you, I hate you, shut up*—all the worst things. John couldn't keep himself from giving advice instead of saying what I was asking him to say, which was, *I know you're having a hard time*. Then, when I told him I didn't want advice, he said over and over and over again, *You asked what you should do during your first day of full-time child care*. All that mattered to him was that he felt right about something.

I took a walk with a neighbor and asked her if she'd been working.

—I've had a couple of small jobs, but nothing over the summer.

—Does it bother you?

—No, I'm not looking for new jobs right now. Just holding down the fort and taking care of the kids is enough. And my husband was shooting a movie in Toronto, so we were back and forth.

She meant that raising kids and running a house was a full-time job.

I met another new friend at a playground. She nursed her wild, roaming, happy boy while my child just clung to me. I wished I were brave like them.

Once the child was down for a nap I didn't know what to do other than clean the house. There was no self left.

Then came another birthday of mine that I didn't notice.

The child and I played inside in the afternoon and I realized I enjoyed spending time with him, that he was my favorite person, that I had nothing left for anyone else, and I felt ashamed.

I was a good wife today, I thought. I'd written nothing in a month, almost nothing in more than a year.

The second sitter canceled, claiming a sore foot. I appealed to the first sitter to return.

The second sitter canceled again. I phoned a third sitter at eight in the morning and hired her hopelessly.

The third sitter arrived thirty minutes late and returned from the playground thirty minutes late, but the child adored her.

The second sitter arrived late on what she didn't know yet was her last day.

The third sitter canceled for the day after that, having forgotten it was a bank holiday and that she'd already promised to work elsewhere.

I fired the second sitter. Before she left, she stuck her chewing gum to the child's crib.

Then I feared that trying to stay a writer would render me unrecognizable, just burned to a husk by frustrated rage. That was the one part of my life, I thought, in which I could exercise choice. Wifehood and motherhood were unassailably permanent, I thought.

The third sitter arrived with a bag of her son's old toys. She brought the child to a play date with her friends and their own tiny charges. They had a picnic at the park and the child came home asleep. In her last few minutes, she did dishes and tidied up the toys. I sat down for the longest I'd sat down in months and watched her save my life.

As if to remind me not to relax, not ever to relax or feel secure, the child screamed and sobbed at bedtime. He hadn't done this in months, maybe even a year. He was fine in my arms, just didn't want to be in his crib. And John was out celebrating his having had a great meeting with Polyglot's investment committee.

Thus ended my forty-eight hours of feeling safe, secure, and able to work again.

The third sitter cleaned and restocked the diaper bag without being asked, and the child was delighted to see the first sitter, who relieved the third sitter after naptime. My heart swelled with the joy of relief—and with the pleasure of being myself for an entire day.

While doing errands on a Saturday, John and I ran into a pregnant friend. She mentioned with shy pride that her husband was on his weekly two-hour bike ride. *Weekly? Not for long,* John said with a grim smile. She had no idea. I'd had no idea.

I was invited to a conference that was three hours away by car, but I didn't think I could leave the child or bring him along without John in tow. John couldn't come. I couldn't do it. I didn't go.

The third sitter showed me photos of the child playing with other children, the child pushing a little cart, the child wearing his little raincoat. It pulled at my heart that so much growth had taken place away from Mama.

John was in Calgary again. I spent all day planning the logistics of our trip to Alberta for his college reunion. It still felt like a temporary condition, my writing only a few minutes a day, and not life from then on.

I ovulated not ten minutes after John walked in the door that night. My body wanted another baby, and it knew my chances of giving it one were slim, so it tried to make things very easy for me.

One day I asked the child, *What do you want to be when you grow up?*

The child said, *Mom.*

In Alberta, in freezing rain, we weren't allowed into John's college reunion because, his classmate explained, he hadn't registered for it. Out of two hundred people in his class, he was the only one not on the list. He explained to me that it was the school's fault, not his, that he'd pre-registered just as everyone else had, that it wasn't his fault.

He kept telling me to stop letting it show on my face. To hide how I felt so that no one would know, no one would be able to read the proof of my shame and humiliation, which by then I always felt for John so he never needed to feel it himself.

There we were, our little family: a calm, reasonable man; a serene, adorable child; and a bitter, furious woman. I let it show on my face. My witchy, nasty, angry face.

Someday in the future, in the darkest part of my mind, we'd lose our house, and our child would be taken away, and John wouldn't for a moment believe he'd done anything wrong.

Three days later we were packed and ready to leave. John declared we'd just leave the rented crib and play table outside the building, which voided the warranty, rather than asking a neighbor to let the rental service into the house. John was afraid to ask for help. While he talked over me I shouted, *Stop it*. The child ran over and put his head in my lap. I took a tranquilizer, but the damage was done.

———

While John was in Korea, meeting with potential Polyglot investors, he distributed the gifts I'd wrapped in culturally appropriate colors, in culturally appropriate number. When

John got home he told me that a Korean engineer had asked him, *Did a Korean wrap these?*

Then he had to go to the store because he'd left his phone charger, fifty dollars' worth of art magazines, and the three guide books I'd overnighted to him in a Seoul taxicab.

The child picked up his marimba mallet and said, *Lollipop*. It did look like a lollipop. Then he thought for a moment and said, *Plane. Red*. He'd eaten a red lollipop on the plane ride home from Alberta. That was the day I knew he was capable of telling a story.

I cleaned the entire house to avoid thinking about John leaving again the next morning.

The next day he called from Calgary and said that the meeting had gone well, a bridge loan was in place, and new investors were coming down the pipeline. I told him he had to find a stable income source by winter or I'd leave him, but I had no plan, just fighting words.

Teething molars, the child looked at me guiltily while holding up stones to his mouth, knowing he mustn't put them in.

The third sitter came in the afternoon. John and I went for an hour-long hike, got a drink at a nearby bar, and watched a movie while the child slept. It was the best day since we'd moved back to California.

John still talked over me, told me my feelings were stupid, blamed our fighting on me, left the room in the middle of a conversation, and said it was a reasonable reaction to my being crazy.

He laughed while reciting the words of an apology. He seemed terrified that if he apologized in earnest for something he'd done accidentally, he'd die.

The laugh—sometimes I told him to stop, but addressing the laugh only gave it more power, and he kept laughing, kept knowing that he could light the fire of my rage. One night in the dark, after I asked him to get out of bed and watch his movie in the other room so I could try to sleep, I brandished my water bottle and told him, begged him, please, to get away from me, for if he didn't I would beat his head until it was bloody.

The next day, the child counted to six unprompted, pointing to the hanging lamps in the kitchen.

The gastroenterologist expressed concern at the narrow gauge of my stools. Was I full of tumors? I asked John to give me a rectal exam. We watched a teaching video online. I positioned myself at the end of the bed. John put on his reading glasses and said, *You'll feel a finger inside your rectum. Just be aware that one of my fingers is a lot bigger than the other fingers,* and then I was laughing so hard that I screamed when he touched my asshole, and we had to call it off.

The next night, I scooted to the edge of the bed and didn't laugh. John said he couldn't feel any tumors.

But I couldn't sleep. *You should be asleep by now,* John said tenderly at one in the morning.

Then he left for Calgary very early.

Later in the morning the child fell out of bed. I rushed in. He said *fah dunn* five hundred times. Then we made a litany of it.

—*What happened when you fell down?*

—*Mama tum in.*

—What happened when I came in?

—Pit up.

—What happened when I picked you up? [silence] *You were OK. And why were you OK? Because you're brave.*

When the child woke from his nap, the first thing he said was *fah dunn*. My heart broke.

I turned the open side of the bed to the wall and prayed he didn't try to stand up, slip between crib and wall, panic, and break his shins.

I stayed up most of the night worrying, but in the morning he was sitting happily in his bed.

John came home and I couldn't believe how lucky I was to have such a happy family. It wasn't happiness; it was the temporary cessation of pain. But I wouldn't know that for another seven years.

John had started a business that failed, moved us across the country three times, and maintained an art practice that consistently lost money, demanded even more travel, and involved lost and broken shipments I then had to chase.

Each morning I woke up and looked at my to-do list and said aloud, *Good thing I don't have a job*.

The child woke up one night, sobbing and heaving. I went in and John followed. It took half an hour of soothing and a dose of ibuprofen to get the child back down. He was teething and drooling a waterfall. I told him the medicine was making him feel tired and good. That he had to help the medicine do its job. Eventually he said, *Put in,* to put him in the crib, and I did, and he lay down and shut his eyes. John looked amazed.

The next day I found an old tub of Play-Doh in a desk drawer. I made the child a little clay pig and a few little clay grapes, which he gave the pig to eat. The pig grew bigger when he ate his food. That day I made four pigs.

Then the child took a nap, thank heaven. It was hot and my hands and feet tingled in the car home from the park, as they did at the beginning of every autoimmune relapse, and John just put his hand on my thigh and I knew we'd be all right. I didn't know anyone else I'd rather have been with during a relapse. I was a lucky person, so unimaginably lucky. And it might not be a relapse at all; it could just have been hot in the car.

———

Then I left for my first solo trip as a mother, to a college in Pennsylvania. A chest cold had made me hoarse.

A woman spoke to me at the Newark airport. *You're a busy bee, there, with that laptop! I thought you must be a writer!* She gave me her card, which contained an Ephesians verse that she told me was the Spiritual Armor prayer.

Put on the full armor of God, says Ephesians.

But I use it as a daily prayer, she said. She also recommended an herbal medication for recovering my voice.

When we got off the pond hopper in Harrisburg, I told her goodbye. *I hope you'll be able to get the medicine,* she said. *But I prayed that you wouldn't need it.*

Wearing the full armor of God, I did my craft talk and ate a salty dinner and read and signed books and answered many questions. No coughing or fever all afternoon.

Then I came down with pinkeye and began to weep green goo.

I woke at three in the morning and coughed up most of what was left in my chest. I got eye drops at the airport. The full armor of God.

I sounded like a woman who liked to smoke and speak loudly in bars. People seemed to assume that I was friendly. With my new voice, I was likable. People asked questions that led to small conversations I would have rolled my eyes at a week earlier. Grateful that I could make any sound at all, I felt it was a pleasure to speak.

I wrote to Hannah, *I just had the most mind-bending trip to Pennsylvania. I met a capuchin monkey and got pinkeye.*

The night I came home, I coughed so hard I was afraid I'd give myself a stroke.

I felt relieved but sad that John had been able to care for the child without me. He grimly said, *We survived three days. When some scientists were able to cure a mouse of a tumor, they said, "Don't overestimate what we've been able to do here. We haven't cured cancer. We cured one kind of tumor in one mouse."*

As if in response, the next day, the cold virus triggered my autoimmune disease, which had been in remission for seventeen years. My feet went numb. My ability to walk and breathe began to fade.

Diaphragm and hip flexors weak, I got admitted through Emergency in minutes.

John looked terrible.

My walking was quite bad by the third day. Seventeen years ago, it hadn't been until day nine.

I needed to get through the infusion so I could go home and take care of the child.

After the first day of the infusion my walking continued to deteriorate. My diaphragm still seemed weak. I kept my eye on the target, which was getting well fast and going home to be the child's mother.

By the third day my cough was almost gone, my diaphragm stronger, but the numbness and hip flexors were worse. My face was already fat after two days on steroids. The IV site infiltrated and I needed a new line. Depressed—on day three? There was no time for that. I swept it away.

The covering neurologist said, *I read your file. It's fairly heroic.* He was impressed by my strength, asked if I lifted weights, if I'd ever gone into respiratory distress. *I've never been intubated, but I've been in intensive care for long periods.* To his ear, my suffering was already legendary.

I was released after five days. The child ate lunch on my lap and played on me while I lay supine on the sofa. He seemed not to mind my not being able to pick him up.

The sitter had cleaned the entire house and left a coconut rice pudding.

John canceled the second in a series of business trips. He looked terrible.

I got down and up from the floor many times. Picked up the child and held him. I could just about change a diaper except for the final transfer from changing pad to floor. I couldn't tell weakness from fatigue at that point.

Depression impedes healing, and I refused to impede my healing.

I walked four tenths of a mile in fifteen minutes, clutching John's arm.

Then the nanny's car was repossessed and John flew to Calgary.

The child brought a funnel into the room, held it up, and said, *Dustpan!*

I took the child to the park. My hands went numb in the sun and I held them under the water fountain, trying to get the feeling back.

The child slipped almost all the way out of my weakened arms as I wrestled us up the stairs to the apartment, so of course he woke up. Then he came running out of the room after I put him on the bed for a nap. God help me. I led him back, and he stayed on the bed talking to himself for a full hour.

The next day I couldn't move.

The sitter out sick, John took the child to the park.

Things would never settle down.

John paid cash to get an abscessed tooth pulled. I had an anxiety attack while driving to pick up noodles at night.

The child looked at my website. *That's a picture of my mom's face.*

I'd started my fifth book soon after I'd married John, and he'd given me notes. The book had sold fewer copies than my previous book. For years afterward, whenever the book came up in conversation, wherever we were, he always said, *You should have put it into chapters. You should have listened to me. That book was a failure.* Over and over again, through months and years, in front of other people, even, I'd asked him to stop, but he never did. His criticism was impossible to reconcile with my insistence that I was happily married, so I refused to acknowledge it.

From that point forward, every time I wrote anything, I worried that John would use it to cut me down. And he did, and I felt ashamed that I was married to someone who seemed to enjoy doing that.

John came home early from work one day, ostensibly to help me take care of the child while I finished writing a book review. He took an hour-long nap, spilled a glass of iced tea on the child's rug, and began to sop it up with one of the new hand towels. I told him to get a kitchen towel. He then put three soaking wet kitchen towels in the hamper on top of the clothes. When he showed me the shitty bread he'd bought at the grocery story, even though I'd asked him to go to the health food store, I exploded and he told me I was overreacting.

I could have worked on the review, but I felt depleted.

Bamboo is getting a change. The child put Bamboo the bear on his back on the table. I fetched a pile of white handkerchiefs and diapered the bear. *Don't move, Bamboo,* the child said.

I cleaned the entire house to avoid thinking about John leaving again the next morning.

When the child got wet and I took him to the bathroom, he whined and squirmed and I shouted, *Stop it!* and he just went quiet and looked away, seemed to drop out of the present moment. Later he broke both of the mallets from my old bell chimes and I somehow had a phone call with an editor while he was underfoot. When John came home at five I'd already had two glasses of wine.

I told John that my editor was leaving to go to another magazine, and that he'd included my name in his application letter. John said, *So now that's two editors who used your name to get better jobs*. I hadn't remembered the other one. I was surprised that he had.

The child insisted on hugging me while he was pooping. In other countries, children were being mutilated by bombs. I had no problems.

John left for four days. I knew it was a privilege that my biggest problem that week was that I loved my husband and would miss him while he worked to support our family.

I was tearfully afraid that I wouldn't be able to relinquish the child's bedtime ritual to a new sitter, drive back and forth across the city at night, teach my first class at a new school, and say goodbye to the third sitter forever while John was away all week.

The child appeared, held up a wrapper of a zinc lozenge, and said, *I found a piece of sore throat.*

John sneered at me six inches away from my face until I couldn't take it anymore and slapped his cheek. He smacked me in the back of the head. I ordered a book about abusive relationships. We never discussed it.

Hannah suggested that John was insecure about my career, but I couldn't change that. The book said that I could change the way I reacted to John's contempt, and in that choice I was absolutely free.

I wished I could just email everyone I knew: *I'm isolating myself because it's exhausting to pretend my marriage is fine.*

The next day I barely looked at John, and he didn't belittle me once. That night I wept.

I asked John to apologize for hurting my feelings, and he did. *Maybe we can get through this without counseling,* a wife said for the two-billionth time in human history.

I gave up a lucrative lecture gig for an art opening that John suddenly wasn't having anymore. I asked him to explain why, and he snarled, *I support this family*.

Our marriage seemed to have sustained an injury that time and kindness might have been able to repair. What could I do? I kept going for the child's sake. If we made it through the year, it would be nine years since we'd met.

This is what I said to my husband that day:

You don't get to call me a bitch and walk out of the room. I am not going to tolerate that anymore. I'm going to be hurt and ashamed that I'm married to someone who would do that, and it's going to splash back onto you. This is no way to live. I don't want us to talk to each other like this anymore. I want to take full accountability for my part in it, and I want you to help me with that. And I want you to take full accountability for your part in it, and I want you to let me help you with that. And if we have to apologize to each other every fucking day from now on, then that's what we'll do. Because I will not live with us talking to each other like this anymore.

He said, *Fine*.

I wondered whether we could return to the behavior of the beginning, when all we'd done was try to find ways to be kind to each other.

The child's teacher told me the kids had all stated what they were thankful for. Most of them said candy or Ninja Turtles, but the child had said, *Mom*.

I floated face down in housewifery.

The child looked at a drawing of a happy sun that, upside down, was a sad sun. When he saw the sad sun, he said knowingly, *The sun wants his mom.*

It will never stop being magical and exciting that you can do that, said John after I played the first movement of the Moonlight Sonata while the child tried to close the landlady's piano on my fingers.

At bedtime the child wanted me to stay while Dad told the bedtime story about the pteranodons. Then he wanted to hug and kiss Dad, and then he wanted to hug and kiss Mom. That tiny person reminded me that our family was good for him and for the world.

The child pretended to be a pillow when we played nighttime hide-and-seek in the dark. When I told him I was going on another trip, he said, *I am a sad pillow.*

The next morning the child had a sore throat. John poured him four times the correct dose of ibuprofen and I walked into the bathroom just as the child was putting the medicine cup down and saying it was too much. That was fifteen minutes before I had to leave for the airport.

By then the child was old enough to tell John what he needed, so I felt safe going away for three days to give a talk at a school in, of all places, Calgary. While I was there, with John's encouragement, I visited Felix and Victoria. Like my old friend Eben, Victoria and Felix had a mortgage and three children, and they held an analogous role in John's life: elders, but the same age.

In the living room, our chairs were set at odd angles. Victoria and Felix weren't looking at each other. Something was perceptibly wrong.

When I got back, John told me that a day or two earlier, the child had soaked the upholstered piano bench with urine. He'd just let it fester. Behind the desk chair I spied a pile of dried cat vomit.

While giving a phone interview, I cleaned and tidied the wreck of my three days away.

The child found one of my hairs on his stuffed owl, picked it up, walked over to me, and gently placed it on my head.

John and I hired a sitter and attended a film screening. Afterward the filmmaker, a friend of a friend, joined us for a drink. I took almost no part in the conversation. John had such a good time with this man we'd seen twice in our lives. He was drinking. I wasn't; I'd had a glass of wine at the reception and knew that any more would ruin the next two days. John held court. By the end of it I was freezing and exhausted. It was much too late.

I sensed that the filmmaker understood the basic dynamic of our marriage, which was that John didn't mind ignoring and dismissing me. That night I went to bed with two sweaters and a sleeping bag and still couldn't get warm.

It was only when I talked to my mother that I admitted how unhappy I was. With everyone else, including my psychiatrist, I presented things as I thought a reasonable person should. I had a history of depression; I was probably perceiving my marriage and life through its lens; I had various stressors, including my husband's lack of sex drive and my total alienation from my environment since moving for my husband's job three times in five years—no job, no roots, nothing that wasn't portable. I was so desperately, furiously unhappy, and I never even knew it unless my mother was listening.

The next day John slept late and then announced we'd go to the museum for a nice lunch. But if we did that, the child would miss his lunch by an hour and his nap by two hours.

I just wanted to have a nice lunch with you, John whined. He'd just wanted to have an expensive, boozy lunch anywhere, with anyone. We went to the museum. The child got a late supper and then melted down at bath time.

That night I dreamt of a parade full of women in dresses, and when the dresses were lifted up, they had no legs, were just floating in space, their infirmity covered by their long beautiful skirts. I wept with joy in the dream, so happy that the wounded and dismembered could be so beautiful and strong. The discovery was a shock. A plot twist, a little gift my mind had hidden and then presented to itself.

Then it was time for us to move again. Polyglot's Los Angeles office was closing. Everyone was moving to a new office in San Francisco. This was a good thing. There were new investors, big ones, from a venture capital firm.

John flew to the Bay to see the house he'd already decided to rent for us. It was in the suburbs, but it had an office for me and a playroom for the child. It was a ten-minute walk from an elementary school.

I was so proud of him.

The child was old enough to tell John what he needed, I reminded myself, and I became more comfortable with taking short trips. During a visit to a college in Texas, I flirted outrageously with an assistant professor who brought me drinks and stood too close to me. The cumulative amount of eye contact we made over two days might have been only ten seconds, but it felt like an entire alternate life.

On the second morning, I went into town with the assistant professor and some other faculty. That afternoon, a graduate student pointedly asked, *How was your morning?* Then she asked the same question an hour or two later, and I said, *I told you, I went into town . . .* before I realized I sounded defensive. *You seem to know a lot of people on the faculty. How do you know my advisor?* I was cool as a cucumber, cool as a liar. *Oh, we're old friends.* We were. But she thought I'd fucked him, and with good reason. I was acting as if I had.

Los Angeles to San Francisco—John drove us north for thirteen hours, including breaks to let the child look at a tide pool and a deer-covered hill. Then we reached our new house.

And then, after the movers delivered everything, and after we let the cat out of her carrier, and after two hours passed, we couldn't find her. I registered her online as lost. Then I found her hiding in a blanket-wrapped chair.

The next morning John declared that the hard part was over, and I just laughed. The hard part would begin the following week, when he went to work at Polyglot and I had no child care in a town I knew nothing about.

At least the kitchen was functioning and the toys were unpacked.

John rode his bike to the ferry to work, and thus began my first day with the child in a new town.

Goal for the day: No crying.

Three o'clock, I was still maintaining.

Then I cried at four o'clock in front of the child.

But I got a library card and took out some picture books, bought bananas so we could bake muffins, unpacked a couple of wardrobe boxes, did a load of laundry, and accepted a small editing job.

The child burst into tears half a dozen times during our half-hour visit to his new school, but three separate kids approached to say hello or share a toy. And they cleaned up the playroom like gangbusters.

I fantasized about going home and finding everything unpacked and put away.

Then I broke a bone in my foot. Wet shoes in the tiled foyer. I strapped on the walking boot and waited for the next undoing.

The child asked for a story each morning as we walked to school. One morning he said he didn't like school *because there's too much kids, and everyone is looking at me.* I made up a story about Little Bear telling Mother Bear the same thing.

Mother Bear asked Little Bear, Why do you think they're looking at you? —Because they want to take away my toys? —Maybe. But what else? —Because they want to take away my snack? —Maybe. But what else? —I don't know. —Little Bear, what are you thinking about when you look at someone? —I'm thinking . . . will you be my friend? —Hmm! Maybe the other bears are thinking, Little Bear is new at school. Will he be my friend? And Little Bear thought and thought about this. And that day, Little Bear made two new friends, one boy bear and one girl bear.

What are their names? the child asked.

Little Bear doesn't know their names yet, I said. *Their names are in the next story.*

I dropped the child at school. When I looked back, he was happily playing in the water tub with a tiny friend.

The next day, the child had five tantrums at breakfast and burst into tears again while walking to school. We arrived late. Then I couldn't get out of bed for two hours. Then I got invited to a fancy lunch in the city, calculated it would take ninety minutes of carefully synchronized cars and ferries, and just cried.

Before I had a child I hadn't valued what people call *quality of life,* and even afterward I probably wouldn't have been able to explain to a bachelor friend why it was valuable. My main objective was to maximize my child's quality of life and our time spent together as a family, but to unattached people it probably sounded like a consolation prize.

Tantrum after school, sobbing and heaving all the way home. When we got inside, the child told me to sit down, put my legs down, and then he sat against me and cried. I tried to rock him. —*Don't move! Don't talk!* After a long time, he said, *Can you wipe my tears?*

We returned from the bathroom and found the cat sleeping on a pile of clean laundry. He asked, *Can I stay here with the kitty?*

He curled up on the laundry and leaned over the kitty, just looking at her. After a minute he asked for some popcorn.

I'd been reading Philip Larkin, but at that moment I was so tired of his incessant gloominess. If he'd had to raise children he'd have had to make up little stories and plan surprise treats and give up his favorite indulgence.

John's life had long ago disappeared into his job, where he got to tell people what to do all day and blame them when things went wrong. My own life had disappeared into motherhood and wifehood. We were both exhausted. He thought it was a hilarious personal quirk that I could only shit at night by then, after the child was in bed and the chores were done. He didn't realize that I didn't have time to shit during the day. He still shitted like a bachelor, whenever and for however long he liked.

Those days, when John ignored and dismissed me, my mind told me I felt bad because I'd gained weight, or because of a bad book review. I refused to look at the real reason.

After naptime the child asked for *the fish movie*. Before we started, he gave me his Nemo softie and said, *Can you hold Nemo and be his mom?* I held the fish. Several times, while we watched Nemo in distress, the child pressed the little fish harder into my lap.

Then he caught a chest cold and I spent the day at the pediatrician while John flew to Calgary for the rest of the week.

I kept the child home from school a third day, with an extra-long nap, just to be sure he didn't return to school feeling run-down. I'd rather have lost another day of work than overtax his little body. I spent—it was so hard not to say *wasted*—the day being a mother and not a writer.

———

John left for another four-day trip and I took to bed. The child was dazed with grief. But at least John provided for the family, and at least we all loved each other, and at least we all had our health.

I met a new friend for lunch and drank a glass of wine and then heard myself say to her, *I think my marriage might be over*. I cried pathetically.

———

Whose birthday was it when the animals came to school—was it Harper's birthday?

The child looked at me as if I were an idiot and said, *It was the* animals' *birthday.*

When my parents visited, we played cards every night. As we played I imagined what it would be like after my parents were dead, the family card games over, John at the funeral trying to tell a funny story about playing cards with my parents. It was as if I couldn't enjoy a story until all suspense was resolved.

By then there were several men in my life whose sole function was to praise. My husband was not one of them.

A well-paid teaching gig was available in Los Angeles next spring. I'd have had to go back and forth from the Bay a dozen times. John said it wasn't worth it. I asked him what it would look like for me to work, then, since he was so keen on my earning money. For a moment, he seemed to understand.

I separated the pieces of the child's hamburger on his plate. —*Don't do that for him,* John said. *He can do that.*

The child wanted to be excused but didn't want to excuse himself, and John brusquely gave him a time-out. I told John I didn't like the proximity of snapping at Mom and then punishing the child, getting mad at me and taking it out on the kid. Then we fought about that long enough for the child to fall asleep on his bed, clutching his stuffed panda. It was hard to wake him up.

John sulked all evening and I realized I didn't care what he thought of me or even how he treated me, as long as the child didn't see or know. Fourteen more years until college. But even until then, I was free.

John didn't just need to win the fight; he needed me to agree that it was my responsibility never to say anything that might make him feel as if he'd ever done anything wrong. Feeling that he'd done something wrong really threatened his sense of entitlement.

The child and I spent the next day together. He took his tricycle for a ride around the block, steering straight the whole way. With only a bit of coaching, he did his jigsaw puzzle. When it was time to pick up toys, he put his cars and trucks in the bin and quietly said, *I'm making good choices today.* We read several pages of his picture dictionary. I played him some Mozart.

The child spread his knees wide on his chair and said, *I am an A. I am a baby A.*

When did I get this? The child began to ask for the story of how he'd come to own each one of his toys. He knew there was once a time before he'd had everything. That things were distinct from other things. That interesting things had happened before he remembered time starting.

While describing to John what I had to do now that we'd received yet another different form letter from the IRS claiming we owed another debt, I laughed until I lost my breath.

When I heard the humidifier gurgle I woke violently, convinced my husband was vomiting, but he was asleep. Then I lay back down and felt embarrassed because my heart was beating so loudly. I turned away so that John wouldn't hear it.

The next day I spent two hours uploading files John had forgotten to bring to work.

I calculated that I'd earned twenty grand the previous year, more than enough to cover child care, but John had earned eight times that. I felt worthless, useless, miserable, good-for-nothing.

John resisted the idea of putting the child back into night diapers. The child soaked his bed three nights in a row. On the morning after the third night, John asked if we had any freshly baked muffins for breakfast, and I just laughed.

People without children asked me if I was happy there, in the suburbs, whether I missed living in a city, and I didn't know how to answer because the very premise of that question depended on an ability to conceive of my personal happiness as independent from the need for health insurance, John's income, a good school district, and the other needs of my family, which was logically impossible.

It was similarly impossible to conceive of belonging to my old choir, one of the great joys of my life, separately from returning to my entire old life in New York, one in which I was free to spend many hours away from the apartment. *In which I was free.*

The conversation seemed to be about freedom, and when I explained that I couldn't conceive of my personal happiness independently from the various needs of my family, these people without children correctly judged that I was describing the opposite of freedom, which is restriction, which, as everyone knows, is bad, while freedom is good. But something happened when we ended the argument there; something happened after that final conclusion, for I was a logical person, and I chose restriction, over and over, because it felt good. It felt good to love and take care of the child, to love and support my husband, despite the restrictions on my apparent freedom.

So there really was no feeling that wasn't part of a matrix of feelings; and there really was no decision that wasn't part of an array of decisions.

That love that parents describe as greater than other loves is a one-way love like the love you feel for a crush you cannot even look at, cannot even breathe near. I'd felt this sort of love fully when I was eleven, and fairly consistently for the past thirty-odd years since then. With the child, I felt it again, an all-consuming love that asks nothing of its object, but it was different this time, because I could express it freely and inhabit it totally, shamelessly.

After he pulled the leg off his little rubber crab, the child felt sad. I told him the broken leg was like Nemo's lucky fin. He was still sad, so I told him the story of our kitty.

Do you know why the kitty has a brown spot on her nose? She used to have a rash there.

I told him that we put cream on it and that she wore a special hat but still sometimes rubbed her nose, and people wondered why we were taking care of a sick kitty, but we loved her so much, and then, when she finally got better, we loved her just as much.

And you'll love your crab, too.

He burst into tears, really sobbing.

I feel upset, he said.

That big feeling you're feeling now? Part of that feeling is love. He cried harder.

After an afternoon of teaching and a vigorous session with John, I decided that the next thing I'd do was to bring sex back to my marriage. Everything was going so well.

At bedtime, I discovered that John had left the child's piss-soaked mattress under blankets all day long. At supper, I bit down on a shard of glass he'd gotten into the stir-fry.

The child's articulation took a sudden regression. Then John came home and announced that Polyglot was about to run out of money. Investments had dried up. They hadn't managed to manufacture the mirror yet, and now they never would.

We had two months of savings left.

John, rendered irrational from stress, said we'd move back to Los Angeles if he could get a job there. I feared he'd insist we move, that he wouldn't consider the toll a fifth move in six years would take on my health, that we would indeed move, that I would never recover from the stress and depression and rage.

John and I had had a date night planned for a month, but because Polyglot was about to spend its last dime, he canceled. Oh well, we'd gone on a lot of dates when we were young. In a few months we'd clock ten years.

I felt sick when I saw pregnant women whose first children were younger than my only child. I thought I'd probably always regret not having had another. But I couldn't have done it without the stability of a home. I just couldn't have done it, moving as much as we had.

Watching John prepare to shut down Polyglot, I'd never seen him suffer so much, not even when his mother was dying.

John explained that he was an expensive, mid-forties executive, and there weren't many of those jobs, so I should get ready for another move.

It was strange to hear him describe himself as an executive, but he'd been the co-founder of Polyglot, so it was technically accurate. He could present himself as an executive, but he could also present himself as an artist, though he hadn't shown any art in five years.

Polyglot would stay solvent through the summer, but his role in its daily operations had dwindled. Those days he did little but play video games on his phone and sulk.

Then the COO laid him off.

So John had started two companies and gotten fired from both.

I said, *We wouldn't have made it ten years if we weren't funny.*

—*Well, if one of us weren't funny.*

—*Yes. You.*

—*That's what I meant.*

Felix and Victoria, in town for a wedding, visited with their new dog. The child asked, *Can I play with the leash?* Then he ran the little dog around the yard, smiling hard.

That night, in the bath, the child looked at his fist. *I made a knuckle family! This is me, this is Mom, this is Dad, this is the kitty, and this is* . . . [looking at his thumb] *Daphne*. The name of the dog he'd played with that afternoon.

After dinner I put the child through a drill, watching him carry his night-light to the door to go to the bathroom himself at night. On the toilet he beamed. I could see his mind changing. I told him, *You have the power to do this yourself. You are powerful.* After I drilled him through tucking himself back into bed, he asked, *What animal will I be when I grow up?*

—*You can be anything. Anything you want.*

—*I think I'm going to be a goshawk.*

That night the child picked up his night-light, opened the door, brought the night-light to the bathroom, set it down, used the toilet, brought the night-light back. I watched from the bottom of the stairs. He jogged in place a little before going back to his room to bed, he was so proud of himself. And then the door closed behind him and he'd crossed another threshold.

I told the story again as if it wasn't a big deal: *We moved from L.A. to the Bay for John's job. Nine months later he was fired. Four months after that, we went broke.*

Minutes after I wrote it down, John was offered a job in the L.A. office of a big corporation. We'd have good health insurance for the first time.

What new worry would come to take money's place?

Minutes later, the child vomited the contents of his stomach onto the living room rug.

Afterward he could drink a little and take a bite of toast but couldn't finish it. Tried valiantly at a cracker.

I laundered vomit-soaked sheets until the dryer broke and then took two wet loads to the laundromat, which as usual was full of heroic women. One dabbed at a bloody wound on her boyfriend's head. Another folded bag after bag of things while her child ticced and squeaked.

I thought about all the wives who had lived before birth control, before legal abortion, before the recognition of marital rape and domestic abuse, before women could buy a house or open a bank account or vote or drive or leave the house. I wanted to apologize to all the forgotten and unseen women who had allowed me to exist, all the women I'd sworn not to emulate because I'd wanted to be human—I wanted to be like a man, capable and beloved for my service to the world.

But I also knew that the most intimate relationship is not mutual. It is one-way: the mother's relationship to the child.

The best part of my life had been this animal intimacy, the secretion of my milk into this body, the teaching how to lift food to the mouth, how to speak, how to show love according to the feeling of love, how to put on a shoe, how to pick up a spoon, how to wipe one's own tears, how to piss and shit and be clean. Nothing, nothing in the world like that. That absolute authority of which the baby must be convinced in order to feel safe, separate from the mother's body. The honor the mother must give the baby, when the baby is ready to know that her absolute authority was never real. The careful timing of the revelation that, baby, you are alone, as alone as anything can be. How lucky you were, baby, to have been a baby with its mother. Now you are ready to start living life in the imagination, to start imagining your way back to every good feeling you don't quite remember from the days of milk.

I wanted my son to have a calm, capable mother, and I began to think of myself as capable, calm, and optimistic, and then I became that way. That was the order in which those things happened.

I still checked with myself, most days, to see if the child was still the only reason not to kill myself.

Out on a long drive, the child whined, quite uncharacteristically. *My neck,* he whimpered, pointing to his neck. We were on a twisty road. He looked gray. I reached back with a plastic bag. He coughed a little. Maybe I was wrong, but I didn't think so. I took the bag away. *Mom, can you put the bag back on my tummy?* Voluminous vomit. Discomfort in the neck; it's quite a good description of nausea. I was then at fight-or-flight for the rest of the car ride. The child was fine, of course, but his suffering deranged me.

By the time the child was four, I'd turned from a person into the sky. I was what the child looked up at when he was afraid. He looked up, saw nothing to fear, continued on his way.

———

I hadn't experienced uncontaminated time—time unoccupied by vigilance to the child's health, feeding, elimination, education, safety, entertainment, development, socialization, and mood, and the care of the house, including food shopping, meal planning, cleaning, cooking, tossing old food, scrubbing bathrooms, making doctors' appointments, labeling toys for show-and-tell, planning play dates, maintaining contact with grandparents, planning holidays, paying bills, dealing with two tax audits and an identity theft (all John's), and usually most of these things at once—outside an airplane in years. This meant absurdly little of the sort of time needed to write books. My time, which is to say the time that was mine, for me alone, had disappeared. And at once I understood why I hadn't felt like myself in years. My own time—my own life—had disappeared, been overtaken. Which might have been the reason I was so angry, I thought.

John taunted me in front of the child for not earning enough money—not only was he ungrateful that I'd chosen to be his wife and follow him from job to job, but he was actively contemptuous of me. I could have submarined my career and become a full-time copy editor and put the child in full-time daycare. But I didn't do that. I chose to stay a writer.

John did the laundry at the laundromat but forgot half of it at home and brought home what he did wash still damp. He didn't apologize or admit he'd made a mistake. Then he made the child apologize to him for noting that Dad had put his shirt on backward.

One morning the child asked if he could play before school, and I told him he had two minutes. When I went to fetch him, I found him sitting at his playroom table. He was methodically using my hole punch on some green and yellow construction paper, making phytoplankton and zooplankton. He placed each punched dot into a plastic pumpkin sitting on the floor beside him. I told him it was time to brush teeth, and he got up from the table as promptly as an office worker would when it was time for a meeting.

The cat didn't touch her food all night. After lying on the ground in the shade, she got up, walked over to me, and cried piteously for half a minute in a way I'd never heard her cry.

The vet confirmed that she'd lost 13 percent of her body weight. There was a mass in her throat. She was dazed, hardly made a sound for the rest of the day. At night she stayed in the child's room as if to say goodbye.

Hope with me, I wrote to Hannah. But I wasn't doing anything as useless or dangerous as hoping. I wasn't even primarily interested in the cat anymore. I had already oriented myself toward the child and evolved into a mother who helps a little boy through the death of his kitty.

The cat had become incidental, a pebble in the ocean. I'd already let her go to do what she had to do.

Sometimes I thought that if I weren't writing and publishing and traveling so much, I wouldn't be so frazzled, but then I remembered that those were the things that gave me energy. What sapped my energy was running the house and being a wife.

We lived then in a pre-diagnostic twilight, but I knew the cat was dying. She didn't fight her meds anymore and stayed in my lap whenever I was home.

That kitty, that tiny thing, had made me a mother. Because of that fact, I loved her in a way I loved no one else.

I retrieved a skeletal cat from the hospital, her fur caked with watery shit. I bathed and combed her and gave her two liquid medications that I feared would ruin her appetite. She ate a little and leaked a putty-colored paste. I followed her and wiped her bottom and wiped where she sat. In an hour we were all coughing and sneezing. The house was filthy. I felt nothing for her and wanted her to die. The hospital bill cost as much as my car.

After bad things happen, it's good to hear from those who have survived them, but it's better if they don't say, *You will get through this, too.* That omission is the most comforting part. Don't ask me to take refuge in a lie.

And so we were back in Los Angeles. To live. For the third time.

I tried to unpack and get settled with no child care and John at work all day, which couldn't be done.

I shattered the glass in a framed picture and broke a lamp. I arrived twenty minutes late to a school tour. I subjected the child to yelling and swearing and panic because the

GPS kept trying to make me turn left across six lanes of traffic out of alleys with no traffic signals. I walked into at least a dozen doorjambs and cabinet knobs and boxes and pieces of furniture. John came home from work and wondered aloud why I hadn't unpacked anything.

I stopped shaking by bedtime but still couldn't sleep. *You should be asleep by now,* John said, sounding concerned.

The child and I visited a preschool. The teacher read a picture book and then asked, *What did Franklin the turtle do on Thanksgiving?* and the child answered, *One time when I was shopping with my mom she forgot where we parked the car.*

Our new neighbor had dropped out of college to care for his ailing father for fifteen years while trying to have a limo business; his seven older siblings had all become doctors or nurses. His wife was an alcoholic; his son had hemophilia; he hated his job. When he took Vicodin for his pain from carrying his father around, he got into fights. His siblings didn't help him care for his father. He was so angry. I told him to try acupuncture, but then I saw that he wanted to stay angry. I told him a bit about my life, said we'd moved five times in six years and that John had gotten fired three times. He asked, *Why are you still with him?*

That's what most people would ask if I told the story to them like that, in one sentence.

John got up late and took a long shower and I had to get the child ready for school and forgo my own shower. Then we had a horrible screaming fight. He shouted, *Fuck you,* and stormed out of the house, calling over his shoulder, *You've been yelling at me for ten minutes straight!*

Then he flew to Calgary.

I bought, wrapped, packed, and shipped holiday gifts to all the grandparents.

The cat's eyes were glazed, her breath shallow.

I read a famous novel about a mother who goes insane. Were all mothers insane? All the living mothers were insane.

The child's shark backpack arrived, his first big-kid backpack. He wore it that night on our nighttime walk. He picked up a yellow leaf and took off his backpack. *What are you doing?* I asked. He looked at me and said, *I'm putting it in my backpack.*

I wrote down the story so I could see it all at once:

We've moved for John's job five times in less than six years. By necessity, I've adjunct-taught the whole time. John was out of work for six months last year, and it wiped out our savings. Besides that, we have John's tax debts and school loans. Our landlord didn't let us break our lease, so now we're paying two rents, to the tune of ten grand a month. We made stupid financial decisions all our lives, and now, in our mid-forties, we're fucked.

I reread the story and wished I didn't appear so compliant in it.

John had an art show, the first he'd had in years. The gallery was in Santa Cruz, just far away enough that a day trip wasn't reasonable.

John said that he'd hire our babysitter to drive his gigantic framed photographs to the gallery, a babysitter he'd never met. The frames weren't ready, he didn't know how much they weighed, he didn't know how much UPS would cost, he hadn't researched art movers, he had no concept of the babysitter as a human person with agency to choose not to do a job that was utterly outside her purview, he hadn't asked the museum for advice, he hadn't asked his gallerist for advice, he didn't know when the pieces would be ready to ship, he didn't know when they needed to be there . . . and so on.

Then I had lunch with a friend whose husband was her wife. She told me that I needed to write more, and asked me what was keeping me from it.

The cat continued to gain weight on her new diet. John said, *You're good at fixing the kitty.*

I sent the child to school with a sniffle, and the teacher called me fifteen minutes later to say that he'd just come up to her, crying, and told her he didn't feel well. I brought him home, where he watched a movie, ate a hearty lunch, played by himself, and took a long nap. We played a couple of games of Uno. I couldn't work while he was there in the house. I just couldn't.

The next morning I tossed a little origami balloon at the child, feeling grateful that his new school didn't require show-and-tell. *My new school doesn't have show-and-tell,* he immediately said aloud.

The cat took a turn for the worse, stayed in bed all day, and wouldn't eat. There were ulcers on her ears.

John left for a five-day conference and took his car key with him. His car was at the bottom of the driveway and mine was at the top.

The cat ate. John FedExed the car key.

The cat howled all night and I prayed that she would die.

John came home after five days away.

I read a book by a woman who had never married or had children. I didn't think I'd ever have become such a good writer—so, I said to myself, it was all right that the past two days of my life had been nothing but submission to my husband and child. I wouldn't have amounted to much anyway.

After another in a series of fights, I realized that the child was the only reason I stayed with John. Had I started the clock even before kindergarten? Thirteen more years. Perhaps dealing with this much condescension would make me into a saint. A furious one.

The purpose of marriage was to get stuck, I thought, so that one was forced to fix the marriage in lieu of leaving.

When we'd first moved from New York to California, my husband had "supported me," which I put in quotes not because he didn't earn the bulk of our income—he did—but because in order for him to do so, I'd taken on close to 100 percent of the domestic responsibilities and worked enough to pay for 100 percent of our child care.

We'd also moved five times in less than six years for "his" job—again, a complicated term because it was his job that got us health insurance and more money than I could get in my field at my level. That said, I'd never gone a year without earning at least enough for child care and preschool, even when I had only fifteen hours a week to work.

But it was a zero-sum game, by those purely capitalist terms, and if we weren't both made happy by sacrificing things for each other's happiness, it would never have worked. Sometimes it didn't seem as if it were working for either of us. My husband had been an artist when we met, and I had been a frugal control freak. Then we started living in beautiful but expensive places so that he could have short commutes to his high-paying day jobs.

More than any sexual scenario by far, I fantasized about buying a house, building up our savings, paying off my husband's school loans and tax debt from the years before we were married, and making regular payments to our retirement accounts.

My annual Pap smear indicated abnormal glandular cells. The doctor all but told me I should expect bad news after the endometrial biopsies.

John and I had been monogamous for ten years. Apparently the papillomavirus had been dormant in my body that whole time.

I spent the rest of the day playing in the sand at the park and drawing caterpillars with the child. Parties and book festivals felt like death. Playgrounds and caterpillars felt like life. But I'd never have convinced myself of that when I was younger. Back then I wanted men to evaluate and approve of me as they would a man.

But qualified women aren't likable; likable women aren't qualified. The only way to get the job is to be ten times better than the best man and likable, which means willing to absorb any amount of misogyny in any form from anyone with a smile on your face, forever. You must be attractive but not too attractive; men don't want to look at an unattractive woman all day long, but they won't feel comfortable working with a woman much more attractive than their own wives. If you marry a man or have children you will automatically be perceived as not committed enough to the job, while married men with children will be perceived as even more committed, with the assumption that their wives will manage all domestic responsibilities, including child-rearing. Finally, assume no allies, since the other women are competing with you for the few token positions available, and once you get the job, men will be free to harass and assault you with no risk of reprisal. Living on this knife edge will ruin your health, and once that happens they'll be able to fire you and hire a man to do the job you couldn't quite manage.

John worked late in the studio two nights in a row and the cat screamed until he came to bed. It wasn't sustainable.

I told John that I wanted to murder him, and he very sweetly held my pillow so I could punch it a hundred times with each fist. Then I thanked heaven I'd married him and not someone else.

Not for the first time, John told me something I already knew, but he told it half wrong. *Thank you for teaching me what I already know,* I said. *Well, I'm a man and I've been drinking, so I'm pretty much an expert on everything,* he said back. I loved him more in that moment than I had in a long time.

Then the landlord's daughter called to tell us that her father had died and she needed to sell the place. I took a tranquilizer and told John to hide the knives.

Then I wrote the story down again: *We moved six times in seven years, four of those moves with the child, and it damaged me in ways that don't seem fixable.*

I begged Hannah to tell John that I needed to stay in the neighborhood, even though we had to move, because I didn't think I'd be able to convince him of it myself. He'd grown too good at ignoring me.

The cat tore open her ears again but I refused to spend another three hours at the vet and float another five hundred dollars on my credit card despite John's insistence.

Then I spent much too much time reading the internet, trying to determine when the president would nuke North Korea and when North Korea would nuke California and when I would die and when the child would die.

John and I had our usual fight about money, in which he blamed me for not having a full-time job and I explained that it was because I'd moved five times in six years for his job. Then he said, *But if we still lived in New York, you wouldn't have a job there, either,* and I explained that the art school would have opened up a tenure line for me, and if we'd stayed in the Bay, I would have been given a full-time job after another colleague had suddenly retired. Then I said, *But when we go our separate ways, I'll stay in one place for longer than a year and get a great job.* Which was the first time I'd ever said anything like that aloud.

I wrote to Hannah, *Even a decent marriage drains the life out of a woman. During our worst fights I refer to our divorce as a sure thing, impending. Yet I don't know anyone with a better marriage. It really is absolute shit, being a man's wife. I swear up and down that if I outlive this marriage, I will never be with a man again.*

John took the child to the aquarium without me, a gift I felt more than entitled to. He'd worked in the studio all weekend for the last two weekends.

At that moment I believed my husband didn't value me, my work, or my life. At that moment, I wanted out of the marriage. At that moment, if we hadn't had a kid, I'd have left.

The feeling wasn't resolved; it just got set aside.

The child sat on my lap while doing color-by-number sheets from the internet. While we colored blue shapes, I played him "Rhapsody in Blue." While we colored purple shapes, I played him "Purple Haze." That was the best part of the day.

John started making the child an open-faced tuna salad sandwich even though he knew the tuna would wind up on the rug I'd just shampooed. I took the bread out of the toaster and threw it across the room.

I worked on a book review while the child worked on a cutting-and-pasting project for school. He got frustrated with his messy scissor-cuts; I told him that when I felt grouchy, it helped to just work my way through it. I thought it was good for him to see what it looked like when a writer was working. We went outside and ate muffins in the sun. I drew a rainbow unicorn with sidewalk chalk. I blew bubbles for the child to shoot with a squirt bottle. We played Red Light, Green Light and Doggie on a Leash. John painted through all of it.

I needed to make the review compassionate and teacherly, not acidic or personal. I worked on it while John and the child watched a movie about a family of superheroes for the twentieth time. And then at bedtime, John was on a plane to Calgary and the child said his ears hurt.

Unbelievable rage. I couldn't sense what was behind it; it was a dead zone.

A week later, a teacher called at noon to say the child had fallen and needed to go to the ER. The rest of the day I spent texting and calling John seven thousand times while fetching the child, setting my GPS for the nearest emergency room, photographing the child's chin wound, sending the photos to the pediatrician, learning that he didn't need stitches, driving him home from school, texting John a dozen more times, assuming he'd crashed his car and died, calling John's co-worker's wife, and learning that both men had been at the movies with their phones off. She knew this because she'd just had to call an ambulance for a naked homeless man overdosing in the yard where she was home with two babies. *I think our husbands just learned an important lesson,* she texted to me, but I doubted it.

On Christmas Eve I wept at the tree because I couldn't believe it was all for me, the family, the house, the tree, the table and chairs, the gifts from Santa, the sleeping child who would get out of bed soon and open everything up.

Ventura burned in the night. By morning the Santa Anas had blown all the smoke south, so the air was salty and yellow. I drove the child to school; it was too smoky to walk. At ten in the morning the school shut down.

When I said that I enjoyed being able to travel for work again, John said he couldn't believe I'd even have that thought. He said he wished he didn't have to travel so much. He said he always missed us when he was gone.

I got maybe one trip a semester, while he went to Calgary twice a month. I wondered if he truly missed us or if he just hated being alone.

I looked forward to my trips to eat tacos in a hotel bed and rub myself to sleep. At home, I didn't want my husband to see me masturbate. I felt ashamed for having needs.

John said he didn't have a lot of faith in our marriage continuing if, when he raised the possibility of moving to Palo Alto for yet another new job, I said I'd divorce him and take the child.

If we moved to Palo Alto, John would immediately start blaming me for not having a job. And then he'd lose his job and we'd be back at zero again. I was beginning to think that his highest priority was undermining me and keeping me dependent.

The cat vomited into her food bowl. Who needed metaphors?

I thought I'd never write another book or have another thought.

At least our house hadn't burned up in the fires. At least our child ate vegetables and could read.

I wrote the story down again: *In eight years we moved six times and had a kid, and I published three books and won a fellowship and went to Athens with John. John's job dragged us to the Bay Area. We came back. Then our landlord died and we had to move again.*

My internal emergency brake was on, and I couldn't seem to disengage it. Or maybe it was off, and I was just out of gas. Or maybe I was siphoning the gas into a useless, idling document. Or maybe the engine had finally died.

The car wouldn't go. I wasn't writing. It didn't matter why.

I set my phone to grayscale in an attempt to curb my addiction to looking at it, but in my experience there was no curbing addiction; there was only quitting.

On the one day John had to take the child to school, he forgot to pack a lunch.

I was in charge of everything and in control of nothing.

I drove to Hollywood to eat lunch with a newly divorced friend. Her production company had four employees, including her, and they were editing four movies and developing twenty. *I just don't do anything else,* she neatly said. *I don't see friends. Joint custody means much more free time.*

I was tempted.

The vet said that death might be imminent. I brought special food home, but the cat didn't eat it.

I read about euthanasia, feeling helpless. Then I brushed my grateful kitty all over while she sat and purred on the windowsill. She looked better. I felt better. I brought her into the bathroom and ran the hot shower. She lay in my lap and breathed. I hand-fed her the liquid salmon and she ate it. I rigged up some elevated food dishes and gave her another steam bath.

She didn't want to eat again. I felt the way I did when the child was a baby, dazed and half alive.

Then the child had diarrhea, and I was thankful that I hadn't had any more children.

The cat ate a little more of the wet food in the night. In the morning I gave her a twenty-minute steam bath. She wasn't quacking while she breathed anymore. Then she started quacking again. I started paying close attention so that I could offer her death when she asked for it.

John took the cat to the hospital at midnight. They came home at three-thirty in the morning, and the cat was meowing happily. Her nose had been suctioned and she'd spent some time in the oxygen tent. She drank some water and seemed much improved. Earlier in the day we'd discussed euthanizing her.

I sat with her in the humidified bathroom for forty minutes. Then she went out to eat tuna and kibble.

The next day I syringe-fed her. She couldn't smell the food, but once it was in her mouth she liked it. How long would we do this for her?

She stopped eating and drinking and grooming and using her box. She smelled bad. I wasn't sure she could even sleep; she seemed dazed and half-asleep at all times.

She crawled onto my neck at four in the morning, burrowed under the covers, onto my chest, as if to get into me. I couldn't get back to sleep, took half a tranquilizer, slept a little, and woke up shaky.

I scheduled her death for five o'clock the following afternoon. My birthday.

Cats are supposed to hide when they die, but our kitty wanted to burrow into our bodies.

My good, beautiful kitty, small warm weight on my lap on that last day.

I felt wrung out, squeezed empty. I feared I hadn't loved her enough at the very end. I didn't know what she was thinking when she died on my lap. I didn't know anything she ever thought. It was more than I could bear. Every posture I'd taken in the house for eight years was in expectation of a kitty on my chest or lap or under my bent knees. My body was still ready for her. It was so deep in my body that without her little warmth and fuzz, I felt exposed to an arctic wind that I hoped would please kill me.

I watched videos of her playing and listened to audio of her purring. I sent a thank-you note to her oncologist and canceled her upcoming appointment and her chip database account. I took notifications of flea medicine doses off the calendar and put her bed, her basket of toys, and her food dishes away in a closet. I put the humidifier back into the child's room, swept up the bits of dried food from her food area, and took the lint brush to my desk chair, where she'd taken so many naps. But then I saw a bit of fluff somewhere and wanted to vomit. The evidence of her body. I couldn't hold it anymore, and love her by loving it, grooming it, kissing it, and petting it. I would have to learn to love her beyond the fact of her body. With a cat, who cannot speak, there aren't many ways to love other than by the body. I spoke to her and sang her her own special songs. She couldn't hear me anymore.

The house was empty, quiet, and clean.

As ever, her hairs, mostly her orange undercoat, speckled my sweater. I didn't roll them off with the lint brush. Someday they would all be gone.

The child had been saying for weeks that he'd have a surprise for us on March 1. That night he announced that it hadn't come true.

I was going to turn into a cat, he said.

I suggested that people don't really change species, and he said, with a sly smile, that his friend had. *—Her nails were curling and she was turning into a cat.*

—Are you sure she wasn't just using her imagination?

He nodded.

John was in Calgary for three days. The child was in school. The cat, dead. I was alone for the first time in years, a trancelike solitariness.

I slept so well when John wasn't there.

Over the weekend I took the child to see the meteorites in UCLA's geology building. Then we went to the library and got a book about meteorites. Then we went to the store for cream and made fudge—igneous rock!

I wrote down the story of my life again: *Managing the household falls entirely to me, since John works full-time and travels frequently, so I teach part-time and spend my days trying to fit ten pounds of shit into the proverbial five-pound bag. I long for a bigger bag or less shit; it's been more than six years since the child was born, and I still feel surprised and confused.*

Felix was in town again, visiting friends. John gave the child a cookie before dinner and then shook him upside down immediately after he finished eating it. And since those last two things happened almost every day, I blew up in front of Felix. I was worn out.

I told Felix about the artist residency I'd been awarded and couldn't attend, and realized I was furious about it. He said that he and Victoria could come down from Calgary for a couple of days apiece and make everything work so I could travel. There it was again, the unspoken brotherly loyalty. Felix would go out of his way to help me because I was

John's wife, the kin of his kin. John would never have thought to ask. I was so angry. I hadn't realized until then how angry I was. I was about to shatter.

Then the child fell down and knocked out his front tooth in two pieces. His lower lip looked like a ham. Blood everywhere. I became an ocean of calm for him, but once he was in bed I felt as if I'd been through a woodchipper.

Everyone I knew told me that John was putting too much on me, demanding that we live in a house with a built-in art studio for his dormant art career.

I knew I needed to stay alive for the child, but would it have been better for him to have a dead mom than a sad, exhausted mom incapable of loving him enough?

I called John at work and sobbed and screamed at him and then sobbed some more.

Then the oncologist called to report that cancer cells had been found on my cervix.

Hannah said she'd teach my class if necessary. Eben said he'd pick the child up at camp. My mother said, *I don't know what to say.*

The child still believed in the tooth fairy—he came in to show me the little pink hedgehog eraser and four quarters I'd tucked under his pillow.

So then I had cancer.

John was being very kind to me.

If the margins were clean around the resection, then I might be fine for a long time. I tried to think of it as just a simple, annoying but manageable surgery. Then I read a study indicating that 20 percent of removed uteri had additional adenocarcinoma lesions and that total hysterectomy was the only sensible response.

The child cried when he couldn't finish his math dot-to-dot. Then he went into his room and put a note on the door that said *Time Out*. I went in after a few minutes and he was calmly working on a Lego project like a self-knowing god.

When John asked if I could start selling the five hundred books I was reviewing for a prize or if we were going to have to move all of them to the new house I exploded. *That's the detail you're concerned about?!*

John spoke on the phone to his stepfather. *No, we don't have a place to live yet. Yes, her folks know.* It all sounded quite hilariously bad.

I decided not to go wide with the cancer information unless the margins didn't turn out clean.

I decided to go to my teaching residency unless I was hemorrhaging.

Days after a right-wing nutjob posted on social media that all journalists should be murdered, five people were shot to death inside a newspaper office. That was the day I gave up and accepted that I'd be shot someday. Until then I could only try to set an example for the child.

I decided to tell the child on Sunday, *Tomorrow I'm going to the doctor and having a little operation called a biopsy. Dad will pick me up at the doctor, and you'll wait here with the sitter. I might be tired for a couple of days, and then for about a month I won't be able to lift heavy things or swim. But after that I'll be all better.*

The script settled, I had an excellent presurgery session with John.

I was light-headed and short of breath from the anesthesia but had little pain. I probably shouldn't have made the child his breakfast and lunch, but I wanted him to feel that things were normal.

Eben found out that his wife had been cheating on him. He said that the clearest indication of cheating was contempt on the part of the cheating spouse. I took half a tranquilizer. My hands were shaking.

John and I were gentle and kind with each other while I healed. I felt safe enough, five weeks after surgery, to touch the place where my cervix used to be. It was hollow, a dome ceiling, no longer a knob.

John wanted the child to go to an elementary school with no grades. I started to say, *I don't want him to turn into . . .* and then John said, *a handsome executive at one of the largest companies in the world, after having started two companies and shown art at one of the most significant museums in the country?* and we both started giggling.

But he wasn't an executive; he was a manager. His companies had failed, and his once nascent film career had run aground.

And I was a woman who had tied her wagon to this man. I'd been persuaded to live off the fruits of his late-stage capitalist privilege. I'd chosen to have a child with him, and then I'd chosen to stay because I'd thought we were a team. Because I'd wished we were a team.

I listened to Eben talk while I cleaned the house. He'd found two secret credit cards.

I spent six hours in the ER after the child vomited his antibiotics. He had a fever and tonsillitis. He got fluids, steroids, antinausea medicine, more antibiotics, and a suppository painkiller, and we came home exhausted. About to shoot into orbit under the pressure of my anxiety, I took two tranquilizers and slept poorly.

The next day I brought the child to the doctor and insisted on two big intramuscular shots of antibiotic to finish the course. Science bless this boy, the organism into which I would empty every last living breath of me.

When you go back to school you can tell everyone about the hospital! —I don't want to. Eyes full of tears.

I took the child to the beach for lunch and as soon as we arrived he started crying, said he was tired, and asked to be brought home for a nap.

Aflame with fear and exhaustion, I tried to nap but only just managed to push myself below the surface, while real sleep waited at the bottom of the lake.

John and I looked at the new house while the child was in school. The biggest bedroom was on the second floor, all by itself. Should we take that room? Should the child go in the front room or the back room? It all came down to acoustics. John went upstairs and I stood in the back room, and he made sex sounds. *Sock it to me! Yeah, baby!* Laughing. It was the hardest we'd ever laugh together.

I rushed around unpacking while John and the child played, and then John said, *Take a breath.* He chided me for juggling twenty tasks while he sat in front of his laptop. I explained that I didn't need him to tell me to relax while he watched me doing everything. —*Get off your fuckin' high horse,* he said.

John built four raised beds and planted tomatoes, strawberries, peppers, cucumbers, zucchini, and herbs. He constructed a hydration system that worked poorly and cost hundreds of dollars to assemble.

You're just getting angrier and crazier, John said, watching me do laundry and dishes and pay bills and apply to refinance his school loans. *Just stop.* I stopped.

John began the day by asking the child, *Do you want to ride your bike or walk to school?* We hadn't practiced biking yet, and walking would exhaust the child, who had gotten wet at three in the morning and needed a change. I said that we'd drive to school and could discuss biking and walking later in the week. John rolled his eyes to make sure the child knew his mother's word was worth nothing.

After the fight, I remembered that moving was stressful and exacerbated conflicts, and that that was part of it. Wine with lunch, coffee with dinner. I'd had the same headache for a week.

The oncologist couldn't locate what was left of my cervix during the colposcopy because it had slipped up into my uterus. She had to tug it down with forceps in order to take an endocervical curettage. While walking with John through the parking lot afterward, I threw up.

Then John went to Calgary.

The handyman came to try to fix the backed-up drains, the broken screens, and the broken door and mailbox. He asked if we had a year lease or month-to-month, and looked horrified when I told him we'd moved in three weeks earlier.

The child burst into tears twice at his gym class. I got on the freeway by accident and then had a second wine. I broke a bowl and didn't remember until I saw the shards in the trash. I couldn't remember words.

You could survive the apocalypse, wrote Hannah. It made me sad. I didn't want to have to survive that.

I even called my mother. She told me all about her infected fingernail bed and asked me whether she should read books by Nicholas Sparks because there were so many of them in the book swap at the condo.

My beloved family and I live in a beautiful place and we have health insurance through my spouse's job, I wrote to myself. *We laugh every day. I get to teach people to read and write better, which is a radical act.*

Maybe John was just beating off to porn instead of fucking me.

Reframe the narrative: *I'm so lucky that I was done having kids before this diagnosis.*

I'd had a great partner, a good pregnancy, a great kid—I barely even knew anyone else with such luck. I clung to my little story. It wasn't all lies.

The night before my hysterectomy, we had a session of great tenderness and love. The man above me was the same, but he had gray hair and wrinkles and wise, old eyes. In them I saw our whole long love.

That night I dreamt of sharing a bed with a handsome white-haired man. We lay in full embrace. I kissed him tenderly on his aged mouth. I loved him despite my husband. We couldn't be together; our lives were already so established in different worlds. But the old man was my husband, once dark-haired, with eyes like jade. I was my true age in the dream, but the old man represented a dedication to mature love, long love, identification with the very old, perhaps an aspiration to be that old, to be with my husband until he looked like the man in my dream.

Hysterectomy.

I made the child's bed and then needed a nap. I kneaded two batches of cookie dough and needed another nap. The child asked how long it would take for me to be better.

John said he'd held my hand as I'd cried out and shaken in the night, but I didn't remember.

The oncologist sent the pathology report: No cancer had been found in my uterus. I didn't need chemo. I was done. Once I realized that, I felt the full, eviscerating violence of having had four organs pulled out of my belly.

John put the refillable seltzer bottles in the dishwasher and melted them because he hadn't read the instructions. He'd put most but not all of the dishes through the washer, wiped no surfaces, cleaned no cutting boards. There was no muesli. The floor needed sweeping. I rage-cleaned and ordered new seltzer bottles.

Being ignored—was that my trigger? For rage and, somehow, also, for desire? *It turns me on when you ignore me.*

For my birthday, John and the child gave me a purple detangling comb for someone with thick curly hair, which I did not possess, and a pack of rainbow hair ties, the same kind they'd given me for Christmas. Happy birthday.

Years ago John had said that my ability to self-diagnose crazy behavior and apologize for it within two hours was exceptionally rare for women. I'd held on to that compliment for years, extracting every bit of its warmth.

Marni, my best friend in town, found out that her husband had been cheating on her, and my first thought was, *I'm grateful that our biggest marital problem is that we don't fuck enough*. But maybe it wasn't just that we didn't fuck enough; it was that as soon as we began the act, John seemed to lose his sense of my presence in the room. He became an actor, and I was his prop, and he was also his vast, adoring audience. He watched himself repeat his favorite moves and fell in love with himself all over again.

I offered Marni our guest room, which was also John's office. John reminded me every two hours that his mother had once housed one of her friends in the same situation. He seemed very pleased with himself. I don't think he and Marni had exchanged more than a dozen words at that point. I heard him talking to someone on the phone about "his" friend who'd just moved in to escape her shitty husband.

Marni said she'd called her husband's mistress and explained that to have an affair with a man with young children is inherently antifeminist because mothers are already financially and socially disadvantaged. She said to the woman that she should get off the phone and figure out what she could do to help women, to be part of the solution.

Marni sat on the floor, her back against the wall, while I made up her futon. I considered the word *antifeminist*. I considered the word *mistress*. Then Eben texted. He'd found a hidden camera mounted in a kitchen lamp.

When I mentioned the book series The Dark Is Rising, John said, *Oh, His Dark Materials*. And then insisted he was right while I explained over and over that they were different series. Then I lost my temper. Then he lectured me for losing my temper. Then he said that I needed to get over whatever was upsetting me and that life wasn't ever going to get any easier.

I put it off for hours, for as long as I could, and then I gave in and imagined how soft around my neck a noose would feel as I hung there in it.

I cleaned the house for an hour while the child and John were at the park, and when they returned, the child said, *Someone cleaned everything!*

John and I both caught the child's cold. John stayed in bed for two days; I took the new kitten to the vet and bought groceries and did dishes and laundry and planned all the meals and took the child to school and so on. I took one nap but otherwise kept everything up. And that is a mother's cold.

I found John outside, picking all the lemons on the tree. Did we have sugar, jars, a recipe? We did not. I managed to get him to stop when he had about fifteen pounds of fruit. He went out for jars and brought home a dozen half-pints. We'd need at least three dozen more. I needed to make the child his supper. The kitchen was covered in lemons.

John laid into me for getting, as he saw it, too angry about things. He wouldn't accept that the root of my anger was that he dismissed and ignored me.

When my psychiatrist asked, *I know you don't take it every day, so how should I write your prescription?* I said, *Just write, "Please give Jane all the tranquilizers she wants" and then sign it.*

Victoria was in town for a conference and came over for dinner. After she left, John said, *You tend to act weird around my friends.*

That night, for the thousandth time, I told John I needed him to have sex with me. He launched right into a list of reasons he wasn't obligated to have sex with me, including that most people our age didn't have sex anymore and that novelty was a big part of it. He thought he'd successfully argued that my humiliation was unreasonable, irrelevant, and wrong.

I went to bed migrainous and leaking tears.

Marni and Eben kept telling me more horrible details of their spouses' cheating. I couldn't bear the weight of them. I tried to tell John some of them, but telling him made me cry.

On our tenth anniversary we went out to dinner and then decided to drive through Topanga. I became immediately carsick while begging John not to speed around every single curve, and as usual he seemed to take the curves ever faster while telling me that it was more important that there were people behind us and that he couldn't drive under the speed limit.

While I was trying not to vomit, John brightly said that someday I'd probably grow out of my motion sickness, which was demonstrably worsening by the year, and then I told him to stop talking because he was using Stupid Mouth. Then he seethed, spitting mad, accusing me of screaming at him and the child every day, all the time, though he could give zero examples of the latter, and I told him that his condescension and dismissive attitude made me angry, and then he said he couldn't have sex with me if I was angry. *I'm scared,* he said.

He sounded as if he'd do anything to save our marriage—anything but curtailing his arrogance or going to a single session of individual or marital therapy or apologizing for anything ever.

I was ready. I knew why people divorced. But who would care for us in our old age?

In the morning he wouldn't speak to me. I felt that I might vomit.

I sent him an email asking for his availability for couples counseling, and he cornered me in the kitchen and made me cry.

I put on the necklace he'd given me for our tenth anniversary. I decided to wear it every day, to remember that our marriage, oh, that holy thing, was worthy of saving.

John bought two enormous wood panels and built a wall to hang them on, in the garage, and then covered them with black paint.

That night at dinner, he said, *I've created a completely new way of drawing.*

He sent pictures of the panels to his gallerist, who didn't respond. When would she write back? I encouraged him to call her, but he just nodded and didn't say anything more about it.

The child was sitting with us when I told John that he was acting as if he hated me. I'd never seen John's face look so angry. Apparently he didn't want the child to think that he hated me. That was the secret he didn't want anyone but our friends to know.

I cleaned the house vigorously and wrote a thousand words. I told my father that I was applying for a full-time administrative job, and he asked why. *To make more money,* I said. *John wants me to make more money.*

—But you're already making money and being a mom. What more can you do? Taking that job would scuttle my writing income and also effectively end my writing career. My father knew, but I didn't know yet, that John's fondest wish was that I'd do exactly that.

Those days, after I went running and reappeared in the living room, sweaty, in my workout bra and shorts, John immediately proposed that we fuck. It was a good incentive to go running after dinner.

One night he reminded me that Victoria and her son were coming to stay with us that weekend, and that we couldn't fuck while they were in the house. I was puzzled; we weren't exactly the sort of people who fucked in the presence of houseguests.

Victoria visited us with her son. They were looking at colleges. Felix had stayed in Calgary with their daughters.

We all went to a bike shop so the son could look at fixed-gear bikes. John took photos of our boys together, one ten years older than the other. We went to a bookstore and bought the boys comics.

After the trip, Victoria's son sent the child some of his old comic books. The child stayed up late reading them.

Since the beginning of our relationship, John had maintained that if I cheated, he wouldn't want to know. He always said the same thing when we talked about other people's infidelity: *I believe in not asking the Magic 8 Ball questions I don't want to know the answer to.* I felt the same way. It was so easy to go along; he sounded so mature, so European about it.

John got his tenth parking ticket of the year and I couldn't get him a parking sticker for his car before changing the address on the vehicle registration, and I couldn't do that before he changed the address on his license, which would never happen.

Still I felt grateful that John and I had found each other and stayed with each other and let each other change—I felt as if the perspective of a ten-year marriage was so vast, I could barely imagine how it must feel at twenty years, thirty, forty . . .

Then we had our ninth session of the year. A few days later we had the tenth. We were going to reach my goal: a dozen sessions in a calendar year.

Fresh from a run, I went upstairs and said to John in bed, *I hope you're watching porn.* He was! Short, hot session, number eleven. Too short. Afterward he said, *I might have watched too much porn.* Then we laughed.

When John forgot to pick up the dry cleaning and I blamed him for it, he insisted that I give him credit for trying. *It's not my fault,* he said, believing it totally.

By then I'd started responding, *Nothing ever is.*

John seethed at me until I apologized. For what? I didn't know. He used my not knowing as evidence of the gravity of the offense. Then I figured it out: My offense was having failed to give him credit for picking up the cleaning after he'd failed to pick up the cleaning.

John read the draft of my new book and said the whole thing needed restructuring on the level of the paragraph, and I fell into a pit. I couldn't do a push-up, I had prediabetes, and I'd never earned any money. Without the new book I had nothing and was nothing.

I couldn't accept it. Then I decided that the book was done. I sent it to my agent.

When I placed a piece of honey toast in front of him, the child said, *Thanks, Mom,* in the sweetest, softest voice. While I read on the sofa he came up and wrapped his arms around me and quietly said, *BLMB,* which means *Bear loves Mom Bear*. At ten in the morning his sniffles stopped, and when I went to check on him I found that he'd put himself back to bed.

Damp little fever bird, fast asleep.

His fever broke on the fourth day, just as the doctor had said it would.

The child's birthday. The first thing he did was write *I made this on my eighth birthday* on a Post-it and then folded it into an origami crane.

John proposed a session and we did it on the floor! He got rug burn and bled on the carpet.

Then my book sold.

I opened a bottle of prosecco and made John dance with me in the living room.

The next day was a dreary children's birthday party. We arrived ninety minutes late because John had ignored two emails from the host. He acted as if this was just the way life went. He didn't apologize to me or the child or the parents, who were already dazedly cleaning up. There was no cake left.

After the party I took the child for a jog. John painted in the garage while I finished the laundry, conducted household administration, and set the child up with a stack of thank-you cards.

After I told John that my two goals for this year had been selling the novel and losing ten pounds, he said, *Do you* need *to lose ten pounds?* So I baked cookies and ate six of them, and then John made fun of me.

I said, *It hurts my feelings when you're condescending.* Then he said, *You're very worked up right now.*

I can fix this, I thought, while he told me that I needed more medication, more therapy. I decided not to initiate interaction with John and respond minimally to his initiations. That's how we'd avoid conflict. My marriage took on the color of sleet.

Weeks into the pandemic, the child's online schoolwork withered to almost nothing. I devised and printed out a homeschooling schedule and hung it above his desk. *Maybe soon I'll be able to get some writing done,* I thought.

Data indicated we'd be sheltering in place for twelve to eighteen months. It was easy to keep my spirits up for the child; without him I might have fallen into a hole.

The child wrote for an hour in his pandemic journal. We baked more cookies. In the afternoon we walked to return library books, but the book bins were sealed shut to keep the virus out.

We walked to the nursery for more seeds but the store was closed until further notice.

I made bread with the child but the yeast was dead so we made flatbreads.

John said we'd move to Australia if everything broke down, and for once I was too tired to care.

On a night we'd agreed to fuck, John stayed up late talking with Victoria on the phone. He was on the sofa in the living room and his face was pink, his expression the grateful disbelief of a teenaged virgin. He was so animated, he sounded like he was on coke.

After he finally hung up, I lectured him about what I perceived as his flagrant emotional affair with Victoria. We agreed to set Thursday aside as date night in perpetuity.

John went for a run and then proposed a fast, reeking fuck. He hadn't been wearing deodorant.

In the morning, the child got out of bed in tears. *Mom, you're usually good at knowing why I'm crying. But I don't know why I'm crying now.* I told him it was because his body was wise, and that it missed going to school.

Then he gave me a hug and said, *This experience is really weird.* What a soul.

I spent the rest of the day on the couch maintaining semi-attentive availability, waiting to be summoned by the child. The only artifact of this work was the child himself, who would accumulate the results of my work in the form of a gradual intellectual and moral evolution. I would accumulate my part of it by looking older and more tired.

John casually said he was going to go for a bike ride even though we'd planned to do yoga together, and I erupted. John was furious that I was hurt and thought I should apologize for being angry. *It's not my fault,* he said, and I neatly finished, *It never is.*

When I asked John to check my busted gearshift, he said, *Move.* Then he shoved me out of the way. Instead of getting mad I said, *Next time, please just say "excuse me."* The child noticed that I was glum and quietly said *ILMF* to me, which was our secret word that meant *I love my family.*

I decided that I just wouldn't be hurt when John tried to hurt me. I wouldn't react. It was already starting to work.

Marni wrote, *This isn't exactly my life dream* and I wrote back, *We're too old for dreams.* Life at our age was about nurturing young, serving community, and, for the very lucky, some battered, wiser form of love, not a dream of love.

I told myself that when I felt hurt, it was because I was carrying damage left from something else, inflicted in childhood, not by my husband. *Look, my wound.* But he hadn't made the wound. And that was my new story.

John said, fretfully, *With this book deal, you're probably closer to being a bazillionaire than I am at this point.* He sounded upset, but why? It was a windfall that would benefit all three of us.

We'd planned to watch the second half of a movie that night, but after dinner John set up his gaming console at the dining room table. He and Victoria had started playing late into the night every weekend, sometimes for five or six hours.

I was doing a great job making sure the child was connecting with his friends, John was doing a great job taking care of John, and I felt abandoned and taken for granted and ignored.

Quarantine had interrupted the world's supply chains, and supermarkets had begun to have trouble maintaining stock. John pressured me to go to a market in a faraway neighborhood that he'd heard had fresh lettuce. Parking was a nightmare, and I didn't know where anything was, and the market was missing plenty of things that we still needed, and people were coughing and there was a maskless man out front, just standing there and coughing, and I had an anxiety attack on the way home.

The worst part was that I'd known it would be like that. I just hadn't had the energy to resist John's bullying, which I knew would last until I broke down and went to the market. He wanted fresh lettuce for his sandwiches.

That night, suddenly ravenous, John proposed a vigorous session.

On Saturday, as on every Saturday of quarantine, the child and I cleaned the house. He got dressed, picked up his room, vacuumed his rug, moved the dining room chairs, and vacuumed in there, too. I did the bathrooms and kitchen.

Then my throat swelled and I felt feverish and borrowed a thermometer from a neighbor—99.4.

Chills. My skin hurt all over.

I had Covid. I'd caught it at the grocery store, buying John his lettuce.

Eben dropped off a spirometer. Showering made me shaky but I could still do it.

The child came halfway up the steps to chat a few times. Each time, he said, *I wish I could give you a hug*. We hugged pillows and smiled at each other.

The nights were bad, with stabbing ear pain and auditory hallucinations that kept waking me up. It was the sound of the child whispering, *Mom*.

Then in the morning I got out of bed, got dressed, put in my contact lenses, and transcribed some notes for the new book.

The next Saturday, I came downstairs, my isolation officially over, and found that John had left the back door open and unlocked and the air conditioner on in the living room. There was cat vomit on the dining room rug. A friend had brought me soup a week ago that John had put in the fridge and forgotten about.

My temperature went back up.

On Mother's Day John made pancakes. The cat played with a plastic bottlecap. The child made me an origami octahedron.

The child needed to make nunchucks for karate, conduct a soil composition test for gardening class, and write a newscast for school. The amount of supervision those activities required was staggering; eventually I would have to do all three things after trying and failing to coax the child to do them. The week I'd isolated with coronavirus and hadn't had to supervise my son's education had been the easiest week of my year.

The child asked me what I was writing, and I explained. Then he asked, *What was your inspiration for the new book?*

He listened to me, and then he picked up one of Victoria's son's comic books and said, *This is my comfort book.*

John proposed that we move somewhere else for the rest of the pandemic. I asked him to summon one good reason to do that, and he snappily asked me to summon one good reason not to. I could feel a hot rage welling up. John seethed. He said he was almost out of hope for our marriage, but he'd started this fight. It didn't make sense.

The child was tearful and impatient with himself, likely because he'd had to get up early for his gardening class. *Sometimes your body needs to cry. It's OK if you don't know why.* I sat with him, sweating ferocious love.

After we walked on the beach, and after I made enchiladas for dinner, I got a stabbing headache and burning eyes.

By morning my sense of smell was improved, but then fatigue hit. Coffee was of no use.

In the morning I realized it had been a very long time since John had held me in bed.

I bought John a stainless-steel spoon engraved *11 Years* for our eleventh (steel) anniversary.

That night John said that his shoulder hurt too much to hold me in bed. I slept on the opposite side of the bed so he could hold me with his other arm, but it didn't feel right.

The local fauna had grown bold during quarantine, now that there was so much less street traffic.

A hawk stood on top of the telephone pole and ate a small bird. With every bite a fluff of downy feathers floated away on the wind. The hawk made a sound like the wheels of a toy car turning very fast. Two smaller birds sat on the wire at a judicious distance, squeaking. They were arguing with him, asking for their brother's body back.

My sense of smell was still very faint.

Then we drove to the beach, where the child promptly disappeared. I started maniacally keening. *If he's gone I will kill myself; I just want you to know that,* I said to John.

I saw a little head bobbing way out on the water. It was the child. A guy started swimming out. A lifeguard appeared and sternly said not to send anyone out, that that's a long-distance swimmer.

A few minutes later the child turned up two lifeguard stations away. He'd thought John had said to meet us on the far rock jetty, not the near one. The child said, *It's strange that I was lost and I didn't even know it.* For him, the experience was just a pleasant walk along the Pacific shore.

We walked on the beach while dolphins placidly swam.

That night, as soon as the child was in bed, John went to the garage to paint. I ordered stickers with the cat's face on them for John for Father's Day.

———

I checked in with the child to see how he was doing with me being in my office so much, and he was fine, seemed amused that I thought he'd be struggling.

Not one of my married friends had a spouse who wasn't impossible most of the time.

Fever and sore throat still came and went. Hives on my legs and burning eyes, and then, as I tried to fall asleep, the whispers came.

All through Covid, I hadn't gone more than a day without working at least a little. I hadn't gone a single weekend without cleaning the entire house.

That night was our eighth session of the year. We chatted and rubbed each other and marveled at the suddenness of our aging—that year we'd both started noticing a dramatic loss of collagen from our bodies. *I've always looked forward to having old hands,* John said.

Before our vacation, I cleaned and vacuumed, stripped the bed, took out the trash, packed everything except John's things, loaded the car, got gas. Then John drove us all the way to Mendocino. During the last forty miles, the child and I both almost puked.

After unpacking everything, I drove to a convenience store and bought Dramamine and ginger candies. Then I drove us up the coast for a seaside hike. I decided that I would do all local driving and medicate the child for long drives.

John complimented me on my mountain driving.

I read sixty pages of a student's novel and led an hour-long online book discussion while the child worked on a jigsaw puzzle and John worked like a madman on a pro bono project for the law firm in Calgary where Victoria worked. Was he trying to land yet another new job? No, Victoria just needed help, and he was one of the few people who understood how to help her.

The outdoor shower was full of banana slugs. The child was thrilled. I went outside to check on him a few minutes later and he was sobbing. The water was cold and he didn't know how to fix it.

After driving an hour into the woods and dosing the child with Dramamine, we failed to find the park John had chosen for our forest hike. He criticized my driving constantly.

So at his worst, my husband was an arrogant, insecure, workaholic, narcissistic bully with middlebrow taste, who maintained power over me by making major decisions without my input or consent. It could still be worse, I thought.

Dishes. Laundry. Cooking. I planned the day and mapped routes to a café, a beach hike, and seals. I made a grocery list, went shopping, drove home, and put everything away. I was a mother on vacation.

I went in to wake the child and he threw an arm around me and immediately went back to sleep.

John no longer touched me when we slept—he used his sore shoulder as an excuse—or when we stood and looked at the stars, or at any other time. It filled me with dread.

Another of John's college friends visited with her husband. We didn't see them much; they lived out in the country, near where we were staying.

Her husband was kind, steady, utterly committed to her, the object of a long-ago crush. It was the second marriage for them both. He was gray and grizzled but had been comfortable in his middle-aged body for at least a decade, unlike the rest of us, who weren't sure yet that we were ready to give up. He'd given up years ago. He didn't seem to regret anything about his life or himself. He seemed like the cool senior, years wiser than any of us freshmen.

I felt good about my relatively youthful body and smooth skin, and about knowing the names and correct pronunciations of *Île de la Cité* and *Berthillon,* but in twenty years, what would I feel good about? What stupid things to think about at all.

I drove a long, sickening path in brutally opaque fog to another infernally boring beach, where the child climbed a little but we mostly just sat and stared at the gray sea and combed among the pebbles. The next day, we drove twelve hours down the coast and back home.

When I was young I'd sworn I'd never marry. I'd understood, back then, that commitment was a trap that closed off otherwise accessible exit routes. Then I had therapy for ten years and learned that commitment was a gift, the ability to give your heart to another. To forsake all others.

Then, more than a decade into marriage, I had to relearn that it's also the other thing, the trap. It's both. I felt stupid, having to relearn something that, thirty years ago, I'd already known. Together, the two truths were heavier than they were separately. I held tight to them both.

I'd started giving myself the sexual release that I needed before bed, with John there or not. At least my body was finally getting what it needed.

The child's old toys tumbled into the giant Goodwill bin—the velvety rabbit with the pale blue jacket that John had brought home from a business trip when the child was too old for it, the stuffed moose from Alberta, which the child had slept with for years and named Millie after his Millie the Moose book, now gone along with that book and fifty other books, but there was no time to grieve; the number of objects flowing into the child's room, even during quarantine, was unmanageable.

The little tiger pin I'd ordered arrived, beautifully wrapped. *I never knew I'd want a pin so much,* the child said, minutes after opening it. And that was the blazing star of the day.

I love it, he said when I tucked him into bed.

The karate master came to train with the child in the backyard. The master said that the child worked hard during the online karate classes, and that afternoon he put the child through his paces. It was brutally hot. The child was dizzy after some back sidekicks, so he came to the picnic table and drank some water. Then he went back out and trained some more. He looked unsteady on his feet, so I called out to him to stand in the shade, under the tree. At this point John sneered, *He can handle making the decision of where to stand.*

The child kept working hard, and the master kept challenging him. I didn't think it would end well. Then the child clutched his throat, fell to his knees, and puked his guts out onto the grass.

John began to hold me in bed with a hand, not an arm; his shoulder had been hurting him more than ever. But he was trying to be tender.

He had known for a week that he was in charge of the child's *Minecraft* session the next day but ignored the inevitable multiple interface snafus, so I dealt with them.

It had taken months, but I finally finished stocking a bug-out bag to last us three days in the wilderness or a month in civilization, and collecting all necessary legal documents to start over in another country.

Ready to pay at the drugstore for the last few items, I realized I'd forgotten my wallet. When I returned to the store with a credit card, the cashier showed me another pile of things behind the register and said that another customer had just done the same thing.

John announced that Victoria had left Felix. So that's what all those hours of phone calls had been about. For some reason Victoria moved from Calgary down near us, where her son was in college. Her daughters, back in Calgary with Felix, were in high school.

I took a tranquilizer before bed and then another one at six A.M. My body was fretful. Every night that John didn't hold me in bed, I expected that he'd be gone in the morning.

Revising the novel, I craved the opinion of an objective judge. But who was an objective reader? I'd surrounded myself with supportive people. I couldn't trust them. I wanted to give the manuscript to someone who wouldn't like it, who would really criticize it. Then it hit me: John.

The day after a glorious fuck with me on top, our ninth session of the year, I diagnosed a vaginal infection, likely from exercising in tight shorts. It had been so many years since I'd had a vaginal infection. I slept with a garlic clove inside, which seemed to help.

John came upstairs and said that the second half of my book was *fantastic*. I was surprised. He'd never used that word to describe my writing before. He stood at the foot of the bed where I was sitting with my laptop, watching an episode of a show about French spies.

Then John asked me how many more minutes were in the episode.

—Twenty-five more minutes. Why, do you want to watch something together?

John thought for a moment.

—Maybe you should pause it. We need to talk.

I shut the lid of the laptop.

—What do you want to talk about?

He took a breath and then the words tumbled out as if they were one long word.

—*I want a divorce.*

He said it with such spooky calm. Maybe he didn't mean it, was just impersonating someone else, someone who could say that to me. His relief steamed around him like a halo. The secret was out.

—*What? No! I refuse. We'll go to couples therapy!*

—*No. I'm not going to therapy.*

He launched into a little speech about my *angry outbursts,* but I wasn't listening. I'd heard it all before.

Adrenaline seethed into my bowels and throat. My face began to tingle. My peripheral vision got shimmery. I thought I might choke on my next breath.

Then John waited a moment—like an actor.

He said, *Do you want me to call an ambulance? Do you want me to call 911? Do you want to go to the hospital?*

No, I said. What new derangement was this?

He'd said it with a grotesque imitation kindness, like a cartoon witch offering me a poison apple.

That was John's real voice. In a flash, his contempt made sense. Here it all was. This was its climax. He hated me. He wanted to disappear me into the loony bin and raise the child with Victoria.

I kept asking John if Victoria was the reason for all of this, and he denied it over and over. I started shaking so violently that it felt physically painful. I swallowed a tranquilizer and waited twenty minutes and put another one under my tongue and waited another twenty minutes and then took a third. I couldn't stop shaking.

I just had to get through the next minute, the next second. I gave myself up to the tranquilizers, willing them to erase all feeling, all thought. I called my parents even though it was the middle of the night where they were. John said, *I don't think they need to know this right now.* He seemed confused, as if I was going off-script.

I told my parents that John was divorcing me, and they asked why, and I said, *I don't know.* I couldn't think of anything else, so I hung up. Then I looked over at John.

You're trying to make me kill myself, I said. Bingo. My tears stopped.

John's eyes glittered with hate. He was smiling slightly, so I knew he felt threatened. I hadn't let him call 911, hadn't meekly held my arms out to the paramedics for my strait-jacket.

I imagined him telling Victoria, *I can get that fucking bitch into an ambulance, no problem. I'll spring it on her. She'll shit her pants.* He'd probably already drafted the solemn email he'd send out after I was gone. He'd inform everyone that I was a violent maniac and that he and the child were finally safe.

He stood there, leaning against the wall, watching me to see what I'd do next. He shifted his weight to the other leg. Then I saw that he had an erection.

He wasn't angry. He wasn't even worried. He was turned on.

I thought I would vomit, but I didn't. John asked me if I wanted him to sleep downstairs, and I said I didn't care, because I didn't. The betrayal had happened a long time ago, the marriage long gone to dust. Nothing had changed but my awareness of it. Suddenly I was very tired. *Just sleep up here,* I said, and he did.

AFTERWARD

The next morning, John left.

I went out back and threw a seashell against the concrete wall between our house and the school next door, and the little shell shattered.

I picked up a lump of concrete that had once been covered in bright cellophane and tied to the ribbon of a helium balloon. And I threw that, too, and it hit the wall and broke into pieces.

I picked up some old bricks, left over from some other tenant's home improvement project, and threw them. Then I picked the terra-cotta bits out of the garden bed.

Was it grief? Fear? Disgust? Whatever it was, it was beyond language. I'd sunk into my mutest animal self, and that animal was in charge.

The animal took me to the building supply store where I told a salesman that I wanted to buy some bricks. He asked me what I needed them for. I said, *My husband left me for another woman and I need to throw them against a wall.*

While I drove home, the bricks knocked against each other in the trunk like a marimba. Carrying them into the yard took three trips. The schoolchildren on the other side of the wall were playing and shrieking. They couldn't hear me sobbing.

On my side, the white concrete wall was marked by the red bricks. Each point of contact, a mark. Each mark, an artifact of a wife's fury.

A wife is an animal.

The animal wanted violence.

The garden was strewn with bits of brick.

Before I could write, before I could even speak—in the beginning, speaking aloud felt as if it would create an undertow that would destroy me—I threw bricks. And so I wrote on that wall the first document of my rage.

Against the wall was my husband's overgrown garden.

I started putting John's books into boxes. We'd never combined our books. I'd never wanted to. Maybe that had made my husband doubt my commitment.

On a call with his father, the child said, *Can you talk to Mom?* and brought me the phone and tried to slink away, but I held out the phone and looked at him and shook my head. I heard his father on the line.

—I'm sad about it, too, kiddo.

—Then why'd you do it?

—I think it's going to be really hard in the beginning, but it's going to get better for the three of us very, very soon. I want to see you as soon as possible and want to spend as much time as possible with you. Do you have other questions?

—Not really.

I took a tranquilizer before sunrise. I was a little shaky by afternoon but able to eat and conduct business. Waves of grief, or whatever it was, swept through my body like electricity.

The child and I talked about the damage our family had sustained, like a fire-damaged redwood. How a tree can sustain damage but keeps on living.

The mornings were the worst. All I felt was fear. I took tranquilizers and cared for myself and the child and the grieving, vomitous cat. It was a good thing I already knew how to do everything.

Eben brought boxes and tape. Nothing of John's would remain in the living room or in the kitchen or dining room, nothing upstairs outside the closet, nothing in the bathrooms. I moved everything to the garage.

I picked up one of John's beloved ceramic bowls and held it at eye level for a moment and then let it fall. It shattered on the floor and I swept up the pieces. I could destroy things, too.

I found a divorce mediator. John agreed to meet with her.

That's great, Eben said. *He's starting to understand what he's done.*

You don't think of a potential life outside your marriage unless you've already destroyed something essential about it. Once you can think like that, you've created the possibility that it could end. Close to the end, I'd begun to imagine that new life. I'd thought it would be like turning a page. But then John left, and I was in an unimagined time.

I felt strong, but then a wave hit my body, and I just had to sit and suffer it. It felt like labor. I sucked ginger candies. I was gestating the future.

The next day I took the child to a play date with Eben's kids, a pandemic rarity. Eben hugged me, our faces pointing different ways. So much love. I wept. He fed us almonds and apple slices.

On day three of our broken family I felt buoyed by love, so much more than I had in my marriage.

The on-call pediatrician recommended two topical creams and an allergy tablet for the child's beesting. I found them all in the medicine cabinet. Another thing John could never have done on his own.

Marni's mother—her mother!—called to say that when she'd heard John had left me but that there wasn't someone else, she'd immediately said, *Bullshit*. She said there was no chance there wasn't someone else. Then she called cheating *a shockingly cruel form of abuse.*

During our first mediation session John opened hot, announcing that he'd had to divorce me to rescue the child from my emotional instability. *I came up with a lot of . . . stratagems for Jane to use when she gets angry,* he said, *but nothing worked.*

I gave her so many stratagems, he said a few moments later, hoping that the word would sound less stupid and more deliberate if he reused it.

That's so retro, Hannah said when I told her.

Then I remembered the story of the great poet whose two wives, notable artists in their own rights, had both died by suicide.

In college I'd learned that the great poet had been saddled by two crazy women who had killed themselves and left him with several children to raise. It wasn't until after the great man's death that the world learned of his strict refusal to let his biographers look at his wives' diaries, which plainly described the great poet as an abusive monster.

Inflicting abuse isn't the hard part. Controlling the narrative is the main job.

According to our phone records, on the day of our first mediation session, John spoke to Victoria for two hours beforehand and two hours afterward.

The child asked, *Do you think we'll ever get used to this?*

I said, *I asked myself that question when you were a little baby, but before I was used to you, you got a little bigger, and then when you were a toddler, I asked myself the question again, and then I realized that I would keep adapting to the person you were becoming, and I wouldn't have to get used to anything.*

Then he asked me, *Would Dad have left if I hadn't been born?*

On the sixth day, the child asked me to sleep in his bed, so I did.

I took half a tranquilizer before showering. No coffee. No more coffee anymore, ever.

Was there such a thing as a therapy group for bereaved schoolchildren? Knowing nothing, I resolved to start one.

Maybe I'd made it too clear to John that I didn't need him anymore, if in fact I ever had.

Maybe his real love affair had been with my financial dependence, and then I took it from him.

The cat was bereft and on me all the time.

I opened John's laptop—a shared computer on which we'd watched movies in bed—and read the last three months of his text messages with Victoria. All earlier messages had been erased. They were looking at houses together, comparing credit scores, discussing mortgages, and referring constantly to a spreadsheet that wasn't attached. They'd been in it for months, if not years. I screenshotted everything.

John's cool, calm sureness had chilled me to the bone, that night before he'd left. I'd thought he'd become a sociopath, but he hadn't become anything. Something had indeed changed, but it wasn't him. It was me. I finally saw that he was capable of deceit.

I walked two miles, guzzled seltzer, and got sick. No more seltzer.

I made a list with the child of all the things he was. A kid. A Californian. A martial artist. *Someone whose parents are getting divorced* was one descriptor among thirty others. Then I asked, *Do you know what that is? That's CONTEXT.* He looked at the list. It filled up a whole page.

No doctor could figure out why my hair was falling out or why I couldn't digest anything anymore but the simplest foods. I hadn't known it yet, but my body had.

When I told John I'd read his text messages, he asked, *Did you read my marriage diary? That would have given you a clear understanding of what was wrong with our marriage.*

Apparently he'd been collecting data for a cover story for his cheating. All the things I'd done wrong that had made him cheat. I did not seek or find that document.

Like a good corporate HR manager, John had put me on probation without my knowing it, drumming up cause so that when he'd finally terminated me without warning, he held documentation to support my dismissal. It would have been a good joke if it weren't true.

During our second mediation session, trying to get ahead of my announcement of the affair, John admitted to having *hooked up* with Victoria in February. They'd made out once but never touched again until after we separated, and that was his story.

When I told Marni, she said, *That means he fucked her at least fifteen times.*

On the eighth day, John called me thirteen times and texted, *What are you telling the child? I need to know exactly what you're telling him. And if you're not going to pick up your phone you need to write and tell me.*

Then he called eight more times. I didn't pick up.

People had started saying, *You'll get through this* mere days after John left, but what I needed most was to be plunged into a massive holding tank containing all the possible endings, even the one with my corpse floating face down in the water. I needed my suffering to be acknowledged. After that, maybe I'd think about getting through it.

During his nightly check-in call, John grilled the child.

—Did you do anything fun?

—We went to the beach.

—Did you get tacos?

—No, we brought a picnic.

—What did you have for dinner?

—Meatballs.

—Did you guys clean the house today?

—Yes.

—Are you playing checkers with the kitty?

—I'm playing checkers with Mom.

On the ninth day, John came to pick up some of his things. The three of us sat on the sofa. John told the child that we weren't mad at each other and that we were going to get along because we valued our family, even though it was a different shape from before.

I didn't want to talk about anything. All of my energy went into caring for the child and myself. If I started feeling anything I'd be pulled under. Anyone who wanted to feed off my tragedy, to suck out the marrow of the details, was getting cut off.

I took smaller bites of food then, and chewed more carefully, since there was no one home to perform the Heimlich maneuver if I choked.

Six guys came over to put the rest of John's things into boxes.

Ten years ago, when John's mother had told me, between puffs of supplemental oxygen, that her parents had tried to prevent her from marrying John's father, she was trying to tell me I'd regret marrying John. I hadn't heard it. I'd thought she was just telling a little story to pass the time. But a dying woman doesn't just tell little stories. She tries to get ahead of the problems she won't be around to solve later on.

By his own admission, John had hooked up with Victoria two days before he'd initiated sex with me for the first time in ages. That night he'd fucked me so hard that he got rug burn and bled on the sheets. He'd been fucking Victoria from a thousand miles away.

When he fucked me from behind, he'd always rested his elbows on my lower back, and every single time he did it, I told him that it hurt, and every single time, including that time, he put his elbows right back onto my back as soon as he got lost again in his private euphoria.

On the tenth day, the mediator called and asked how I was doing. I was cooking. I turned off the burner. She told me that John had just texted her: *Did Jane tell you about her willing institutionalization and bipolar medication?*

I told her I'd been in the hospital once, more than twenty years ago, and that I took antidepressants. I didn't mention the mood stabilizers. She said she'd asked John if he thought I was an unfit parent. Then she laughed. He'd backed down after about half a second.

Then she asked if I'd like John to apologize. I said, *No, because the word of a liar is meaningless.* She never asked again.

My mother told me about all the husbands in the long marriages she knew—gamblers, debtors, and, most often, those who worked long hours, taking unexplained trips, or who slept in different rooms.

Every day I had to write it all down again so I could see it all in one place, but it didn't sink in. I kept having to say the same things over and over. The story came out in shards. It sounded different each time.

I was with my husband for fourteen years. Then two weeks before Covid Thanksgiving he left and moved in with his mistress, who had just left her husband and children and moved fifteen hundred miles to be with my husband. Our son was eight years old.

I called Felix in Calgary. He said, *I wondered when I was going to hear from you.*

Apparently John had regaled him and Victoria for years with stories of my *instability*—the very word he'd used to describe Naomi's problem fourteen years earlier, when I'd first met him. How I'd been *institutionalized* and how I was barreling toward another long stay in a locked ward. I listened and took notes until I was crying.

On the eleventh day, I wrote to John:

Are you and Victoria sleeping together? I realize that I need you to say this to me in order to move on and heal. I saw on your laptop that you're looking at houses together. That needs to come up in mediation soon, for financial reasons.

A few minutes later I wrote:

Sorry, that came out hostile and really wasn't meant that way. I just need the closure of knowing that you're in a new relationship now.

John wrote back a few minutes later.

He said he'd crashed at Victoria's only until he could stay with friends, at which point she visited for dinner on two occasions. *Visited for dinner,* as in a formal courtship.

They were looking for houses together because *a relationship is a possibility going forward.* It was a possibility going forward, like an earthquake, unforeseeable.

If they decided to live together, he promised he'd tell me *before it happens,* thereby removing his agency over it. It could just . . . happen. The grammar of perfect innocence.

My chest started prickling. I wrote back immediately:

John, did you have a sexual relationship with Victoria prior to the day you left? Y/N

He said I'd repeatedly dismissed his attempts to discuss his discomfort in our relationship. I found the role reversal bizarre.

Then he said, *As a result, a space for someone else to enter opened up*. Like a sinkhole. An act of God. Not a clever cheater's dugout.

By then the adrenaline was churning. I wrote back like a lab rat jabbing at its one available button:

I repeat: John, did you have a sexual relationship with Victoria prior to the day you left? Y/N

He answered immediately:

It's really important that you focus on our relationship. Victoria is irrelevant.

A wordless rage welled up, and I began to shiver.

I repeat: John, did you have a sexual relationship with Victoria prior to the day you left? Remember, you can say no, too. Just a simple yes/no question. Shouldn't be hard. And once you say yes or no, you have my word that I'll stop asking.

That time John responded voluminously. Somehow the problem had drifted from his cheating to my having asked him the same question *at least five times*. He was gravely concerned and asked how he could believe that I wouldn't continue to come at him with this *until the end of time*.

He said he was tired of answering the same question over and over, and with a show of great magnanimity and care, he noted that our discussion didn't seem to be helping me or him, or, emphasis mine, *the child*.

Once again, he added, his main concern remained keeping the child as healthy, safe, and happy as possible, which was odd, considering he'd given the child less than fifteen minutes' warning before moving out.

I wrote back:

Just say yes or no. That's all I want, and you haven't given me that yet. Seriously, just Y/N, and then we're done. Nothing adversarial will happen, and we will continue to do what's best for the child, as we are already doing.

My not hearing a Y/N answer from you by the time you pick the child up today will be equivalent to a Y response, as in "Yes, I did have a sexual relationship with Victoria prior to the day I left." See you later.

John sidestepped the question entirely, now that he'd introduced enough adjacent topics to fill a small book, referring instead to my *strange stance* of continuing to ask a question that he refused to answer.

He said that he wasn't inclined to keep answering the same question. Never mind that he hadn't answered it once.

I knew I'd lost the battle, but I wrote back anyway:

I don't remember any of your previous responses to my question because they were just as evasive as what you wrote below. That's why I'm giving you the opportunity to give a clear answer now: Y or N. Looks like you have about ninety minutes.

John wrote that if I didn't remember his *constant honest answer,* he was soberly concerned that mediation might not work. Had I actually developed a serious memory problem in the stress of the last few weeks?

I wrote back, like a good student:

I'm sorry, I don't remember. What did you say?

He wrote back, *surprised and dismayed* that I couldn't remember his answer to a question I'd asked multiple times, as if he'd answered it even once. Why would someone ask a question more than once anyway? Did I not even *trust* him?

John was disinclined to re-answer the question. He said I obviously had some hidden reason for asking the question again, and that I was clearly untrustworthy.

While John typed all of that out, Victoria was probably sitting right there next to him, coaching him, in slimy panties.

I went outside to calm down in the sun, vibrating with a shame so deep it felt sexual. I picked up a brick and threw it against the wall. Then I picked up the pieces of marble John had bought for a project years ago and threw them against the wall until they were gravel. I went inside and got a bag and picked up the marble chips and put them in the bin in the alley.

He thought he could talk me out of things I remembered. He thought he could stand there, his stupid dick still dripping, and open his mouth and convince me he hadn't done a thing.

Maybe Victoria felt like a feminist heroine, donning her armor and shaking off the mantle of the patriarchy and living for herself alone.

Living for herself alone, grinding her boot into the face of another woman, another mother, and secretly removing that mother's agency over her life. While she and John had merrily ordered expensive new kitchenware with the online account I used to buy cat food and N95 masks, I'd remained the meek little wife of the whole disgusting apparatus.

The half a dozen times John had brought us together socially, Victoria seemed like an awkward teenager. It must have been so easy for John to draw her in.

I showed Eben the email thread. When he looked up from reading it, he said, *My first thought is that John is bad at gaslighting.*

I said, *So why is he lying when it's so obvious that he's lying?*

Eben slowly said, *Because he thinks it works.*

That night, Felix told me that exactly three days after John left me, Victoria had told their children, *You need to come to accept John because he's going to be a big part of your life.*

The mediator called and said that John would never admit to the cheating, so I might as well stop pushing.

Then she said that if John had lied to me, he would lie to the child, and that the child would figure out who his father was all by himself.

She added, *Remember that nothing he says matters.*

On the fourteenth day, I hazily remembered what I'd said to John after he'd said he was leaving. *I pity you,* I'd said. *You have none of the skills needed for a real relationship.*

I started each morning with a tranquilizer and an acrid, meaty hangover shit.

The school psychologist found a young social worker who needed to lead a group as part of his training. The child would be able to talk about the divorce online with a group of other third-graders. The group would be called Family Changes.

That night John forgot his call with the child. I asked the child if he wanted to call Dad, and he thoughtfully said, *I want it to be up to him.* Then John called forty-five minutes late. He said he'd been filling out a form and lost track of time.

I drank wine and did laundry and answered emails and did crossword puzzles and cleaned out the fridge and got access to John's credit card and determined exactly which day he and Victoria had rented a hotel room and ordered sushi and fucked.

It was in August, three months before he'd left.

On that day, John had told me that Victoria was in town for work, and that she was staying at a hotel right near our house, and that he would meet her for dinner in the hotel room, safe from crowd exposure to Covid. Even then I'd suspected nothing.

He'd gotten home that night with a ruddy glow in his cheeks. They'd drunk some cheap wine, he'd said. Maybe the wine had been tannic and caused him to flush. But he'd been surrounded by a wet cloud of relief. I'd been glad he'd seen a friend after so many months of quarantine.

I couldn't fall asleep, my body was so filled with adrenaline. Then I woke at five. Took a tranquilizer at six. I still couldn't sleep but by seven I stopped shaking, at least.

I took in all the waists of the child's pajama pants, which were suddenly hanging off him. Prepped financial questions for the next day's mediation session. Looked at rental listings. Walked three miles.

Not even three weeks had passed.

My dream of being in a long marriage, over.

We hadn't even made it fifteen years.

Years and years of contempt, over.

Never again would I have to hide my shame.

Never again would I have to impersonate a wife.

I thought ceaselessly about Eve's deathbed confession.

I could still feel the callus under my ring finger.

I'd loved the idea of a long marriage, like a family heirloom, ugly but important. I'd thought we'd be together forever. I'd thought John would hold me while I died and say, *Good Mumbun . . . good Mumbun . . .* as he had while I'd given birth to our child.

I wrote down the story again: *I was proud of our family and of John's career, so when he played video games all night, spent weekends painting, or stayed out bodysurfing in deep water while the child and I waited, shivering, on the beach, I didn't push back. I multitasked and made my own needs as small as possible because, I thought, I was just more capable than he was. I assumed that made me valuable.*

I took three shits before breakfast and two tranquilizers before the mediation session. John said that he wasn't to blame for the divorce but that his hand had been forced. He described me as volatile and unsafe for the child to be around.

I wrote the word *LIAR* on a sticky note and stuck it onto the computer screen. It covered John's face.

I fumed and shouted and sobbed. I could feel the mediator and the lawyer on the computer screen lowering their estimation of me with every hoarse, sobbing syllable. One of them cut me off. She was scolding me. Afterward I didn't remember what she'd said. Or what I'd said.

Then I cried while the cat kissed my mouth and eyes.

———

A woman lives in the same house for fourteen years. She pulls her old car into the driveway, bumping over the root-warped ground. The garage door hiccups its way up the tracks until it's just high enough to drive under.

She could be almost asleep, so familiar is this end-of-day routine. Some days she frowns at a piece of trash that's found its way onto the lawn. Some days the undercarriage scrapes against the pavement warped by tree roots. Soon the cracks will have to be sealed.

Then one Friday in November she drives home and instead of the house there's an empty lot, the grass knee-high, a chain-link fence, and sun-faded signs warning against trespassing. She clicks the garage door opener and nothing happens because there's no garage, no driveway, no building.

Almost everyone she knows says it's an extremely common thing, that lots of houses disappear like that, and she should just move on, stop talking about it, and find a new one.

After all, it's partly her own fault for choosing one of those disappearing houses. She should have known; after all, she'd lived in it for fourteen years.

———

Years before Hannah found out the extent of her first husband's deceit, they'd been hiking in Maine and reached the top of a high hill. Hannah had felt a sudden urge to push her husband off the mountain. No one would have seen her. For years she'd thought of it as a neuronal misfiring, an errant blip. But she'd known, deep in her body, that he had become her enemy.

The child took another belt test. John was there. His eyebrows had grown wild now that I wasn't trimming them. He said he'd lost seven pounds. *My pooping habits are completely different,* he added. I didn't respond to that.

The child's friend asked him what he was doing for Christmas. *I'll celebrate Christmas with my dad and Hanukkah with my mom,* the child said. —*Wow, did you celebrate both holidays when they were together?* —*They aren't together anymore,* the child began, as if seeing how it would sound, spoken aloud, in his own voice.

Depression lowered onto me from the cloud cover. Exhausted, I drank my first coffee in almost a month.

On a video call with the child, John said he was planning a trip for the two of them. *A trip? I wish Mom could come,* the child said. *It's OK to wish things like that,* John said, oozing self-regard. The child said, *I hope Mom didn't hear that.*

I took the child to the beach on New Year's Day. We piled up the sand and made a sand-snowman with a carrot nose and acorn eyes. Then we kicked and stomped it to death.

Marni said that what John had done to me wasn't nearly as bad as what her sister's husband had done. He'd beaten her up. He'd spent the night in jail. But what John had done wasn't a crime of passion. It was methodical.

Tears threatened. The day lasted a hundred million years.

The consequences of John's betrayal would reverberate through generations, I thought. At last he'd made a mark on the world—as a maestro of dishonesty.

Then I went into the bathroom and stood up straight at the mirror and remembered that I was a mother, a person who could lift a truck off a child with her bare hands.

So many books and movies for children depict a family moving to a new place because their father has decided to return to his hometown or explore a new city or move into an old, dilapidated house in the country. The mother defers to her husband. The words *coerced* and *nonconsensual* are not used.

The man doesn't owe anyone an explanation. The rest of the family wonder privately why he has upended their lives. When the children complain, they are scolded. The mother looks distraught, but she never challenges her husband. If the children are in the room, she smiles and tries to hide her feelings.

Against this background, the children begin a supernatural adventure, the father finds his niche in the new town, and the mother disappears into the background.

John had dragged me thousands of miles, back and forth across the country, just as his father had dragged his mother from Arizona to Alberta. John left me when our son was eight years old, just as his father had done to his mother.

I hoped the child wouldn't do that to his wife.

Then I wondered if John's mother had ever had that thought.

I became a tugboat hauling around a mortifying barge of unwashed sadness. My son stood on deck, frightened and helpless. My breath reeked of the grave. I was inhuman, annihilated.

Early in our marriage, John had said we should make our life decisions mathematically, with numeric values assigned to each category. His art career and day job both got fives. Mine got threes because my career was more advanced than his and my day job didn't pay as much as his. When I suggested that we make these decisions together, John didn't say anything, and the conversation ended.

Back then I'd thought that John was working ten hours a day. After we separated, he was suddenly available to fetch the child from school and do all the errands and chores for his own new house that he'd never had time to do when we lived together. Surprise.

I was still trying to explain to myself how I'd become this person, this discarded wife, when I'd never even wanted to be a wife in the first place.

I wrote in my notebook, *Please let there be a lesson at the end of this.*

The term *reality distortion field* was used on a well-known sci-fi show to describe the way a certain alien species created an alternate world by sheer force of thought.

Two decades later the term was used to describe the mystic energy of a charismatic tech entrepreneur. He was infamously able to impel his engineers to build things deemed logically impossible. The impresario's charm was also a kind of dark magic that made him just as good at stealing credit for other people's ideas. People wanted to believe him.

Funding and launching a company is a long con closely adjacent to lying. The only way to seduce venture capitalists is to convince them that your company can't possibly fail. With absolutely no business experience, John had raised a million dollars for his first company. For his second company, he'd raised ten million more. He'd recruited and employed more than a hundred people.

Time and again he showed me on his calculator app how much he'd be earning in a year, in five years, and in the first year after the product went to market. The numbers—so many zeros—gave me the giggles.

To see beyond the reality distortion field requires something beyond intelligence. When another tech billionaire was asked why he'd never allied with the first one, he said he was immune to the first guy's power, but that without that rare immunity he'd have been swept along like everyone else.

I'd lived for fourteen years within John's reality distortion field. I'd followed him wherever he went, anchored to his money dream.

When he moved out, John had taken the food processor and the expensive Dutch oven and left me our old cutting boards, the edges of which were pocked with mold from years of resting on damp counters. A week or two later, he'd brought me three new cutting boards. I hadn't asked for them, and we hadn't discussed it. I'd wondered if the cutting boards were an apology.

Then I understood that within John's reality distortion field, no apology was necessary. He was on great terms with his ex-wife. He hadn't done anything wrong. In fact, if he saw something in a shop that she might like, he'd just buy it for her without consultation. The cutting boards were an artifact of his innocence.

The garage, his studio, was stuffed with junk. Extension cords, Styrofoam, plywood, his tools, his father's tools, boxes and boxes of who knows what, with packing stickers from three moves earlier, with my name on all the stickers because I'd dealt with the movers and everything else.

And these apartments and houses with their giant garages were expensive, which gave John an excuse, within weeks of our landing in a new place, to chastise me for not earning enough money.

For years John complained that I fell asleep too early for sex because of my psych meds, but I was always up first, made the coffee, got our son ready for school, packed his lunch, fed the cat, and so on. John thought he'd convinced me that it was my fault that I needed to sleep at all, and that that was the reason we never had sex.

One night I'd woken up feeling as if I'd been violently shoved. When I'd opened my eyes, John was already looking back down at his phone, as if shoving me were as neutral and common as scratching an itch.

He stayed up late. Sometimes he watched porn on his laptop and beat off into the toilet. Those nights, he left a brown mark on the back of the seat.

But maybe it hadn't been porn. Maybe it had just been Victoria.

Felix suspected that the affair had started two years earlier, when John had first said he needed to leave me because I was so angry. Felix said that John had never specified what I was angry about. The fact that I might have been angry *about* something would have ruined his presentation.

Marni said she'd never trusted John. *There is a coldly aggressive and undermining silence about him. I worried that it was all about him, all the time. It made zero sense.*

I'd thought the marriage would improve, somehow, if I just improved myself. If I could sufficiently better myself, the fumes of my betterment would form a medicinal cloud that would surround and improve my husband.

John was an incorrigible jaywalker. Maybe he thought his handsomeness kept him safe. Every time he walked away from me and across a street, it had felt like a slap, but I'd told myself he was just forgetful. Whenever I'd told him he had to walk as if we were together, he'd said that it was my job to keep up with him.

I remembered his pride that Marni had stayed with us after her husband had cheated. John must have gotten so hard off her pain, off the rush of his disguise. With each public kindness, he could do worse things to me in private.

We hadn't held the child's hand in years, not since he was tiny, but for the last couple of months before John left, when we'd walked on the beach or in the park, John had held the child's hand tenderly and desperately, as if he'd been preparing to leave for war. I'd chalked it up to pandemic stress.

I roasted carrots, played chess, went for a walk, watched a movie, and made origami polyhedra with the child. He did a dot-to-dot picture of a dragon with seven hundred dots. The kitchen was clean. Everything was clean.

I made fluffy pancakes with fresh strawberries but could feel an ocean of tears at the gates. When I thought about the next nine and a half years before the child reached the age of majority, I couldn't bear it. All the vacations I'd have to plan and drive to, just the sad two of us. But then I remembered that each day was the only day, and I yoked myself to it and dragged it grimly forward.

John barged into the house fifteen minutes late to fetch the child, with no acknowledgment, and grabbed the kitchen scissors without my permission, and I was so angry that I swore at him. After he left with the child, I threw bricks at the wall and then went running.

Two days later, when I fetched the child, I saw that John's house was tidy and pristine. He'd built himself a new shoe cubby, sanded and painted white.

When I tucked the child into bed, he said, *Dad said that you planned the divorce together. He said that you planned it together for two months.*

I told the child that it wasn't true. The child listened. Then he said, *I don't think it's a lie when Dad says the divorce is what's best for our family because that's just what he thinks.*

During mediation John and I decided to take turns planning the child's birthday parties on alternate years. There would be no party this year, given the pandemic. John said that he'd come over so the three of us could have dinner together. If he could make it look as if I didn't despise him, he'd seem like a good guy. *No, that's not going to work,* I said.

Marni called from the road—she was spending a few days out of town while her husband was served with divorce papers. *He said I had to tell him where I was going,* she said, *but do I?* She sounded the way I did when I still thought I had to give in to John's demands.

In the afternoon, after his therapy session, the child said, *I think I'm going to start writing in my journal again. —That's a great idea. It has to go somewhere,* I said.

My sweet, small bear of grief.

I printed statement summaries from all three of John's credit cards and marked all of the suspected affair purchases. I found many suspicious dinners, but Polyglot had paid for all the Calgary flights and hotels, and he could have used cash for any number of things.

The child asked me what the hardest part of the divorce had been, and I said that it was watching Dad get away with lying. *Me, too,* he said, *but he didn't get away with it.*

The child had new bug bites every time he returned from John's house. I asked John to get the place fogged. He texted me about all the laundry and vacuuming he was doing, expecting praise.

I annotated and scanned a year of call and text records. I read all the screenshotted text chats and found fifty screenshots with incontrovertible evidence of the affair. It took me to the edge of an anxiety attack. Then I filed them away.

I managed to make dinner, cooking and crying. Then I started crying at the table and couldn't stop, which set the child off. Then I tried to play a game of solitaire at the table, to distract myself, but I couldn't stop crying and wound up tearing all the playing cards into little bits. Then during his call with John, the child asked him who his new girlfriend was, and John said he didn't have a girlfriend.

I woke up crying at six and took a tranquilizer and cried until it kicked in.

I got the bike rack on the car and the bikes in the rack and the car to the beach and the bikes back on the car and the car home and the bikes off the rack and the rack off the car and I was ready to die. Cried while driving, both ways. The child kept softly saying, *We don't have to do this today. We can wait for a less stressful day.* Strangers walked by and offered to help and I said, *My husband left me,* to explain why I couldn't put the bikes on the car. I'd become a crazy woman rotted out from rage.

I thought constantly about what it would be like to kill John. After I ran through the likely outcomes, with me in prison and the child in foster care, I knew I couldn't really kill anyone. But I was trapped, suspended in a homicidal twilight.

I thought about another celebrated poet, one I knew a little, whose wife had gone crazy and killed their baby and then herself. I'd never once considered what her husband might have done to her.

Once upon a time, a girl was beaten and raped and dropped out of school and went to live in the woods. Between the ages of fourteen and twenty-two her rap sheet filled up and she attempted suicide six times. She supported herself and her girlfriend by prostituting herself. After they broke up, the girlfriend was apprehended and, on a recorded call, asked the girl to confess to the murders. Within an hour of the call, the girl turned herself in and confessed to murdering seven men. She said they'd all violently raped her or tried to. At a court hearing, after a decade on death row, she said that the state ought to kill her, because given the chance, she absolutely would kill again. Soon afterward she died by lethal injection.

The difference between me and that woman was one of degree, not type, which is exactly what I'd learned, incidentally, twenty-five years earlier, during the psychiatric hospitalization that John had tried so hard to shame me for. Those of us in the psych ward were just ever so slightly sicker than the general population.

The difference between John and a fascist despot is one of degree, not type. *Don't try to make your sad little divorce story about the behavior of sociopathic tyrants,* I thought, but I wasn't making it about what it was already about.

Why had I stayed with John? I thought about that old neighbor's question once a week. I'd stayed with John because there was something different about him, calm and still, like a mountain. I'd long assumed that the stillness was a commitment to being an artist, a safety barrier between him and the conventional world. His energy was calm, and it had calmed me. But it wasn't the stillness of wisdom. It was the absence of empathy.

I have tons of empathy! John had fumed, over the years, during more than one argument.

When John's energy had felt evil, I'd simply told myself that I was wrong. That's why I'd stayed. I was stubborn. I'd refused to admit I'd been wrong about him.

Despite my early resistance to marriage, despite my condescension to women who'd had bridesmaids and changed their names and used the word *hubby,* by staying with John I'd folded just as they had. The difference between me and those women was one of degree. For fourteen years I'd pretended that I wasn't really a wife, and that my rage must be coming from some unknowable source.

John gets to lie about me, forever, to anyone he wants, I thought. Then empathy arrived like a thunderclap and I saw that his cruelty was equal and opposite to the ego wound of being married to me. I had my own money. It would last years. He'd needed all that power back, so he'd found a different woman, one he thought he could control.

I'd been crying for two days straight and drinking wine with lunch, but then I knew I could white-knuckle it to bedtime.

I'd married John because I'd thought a better man might leave me. Does every wife make that dark calculation before her wedding day?

The child went to his father's house for the weekend. *Bye, Mom. I hope you don't have any sad days.*

I wrote down the story again:

I spent more than a decade as the trailing spouse of a selfish man who cheated on me and left me for his mistress. I only ever served as an adjunct professor while we made five long-distance moves in less than seven years to support his career, and I am now forty-seven, divorced, and stuck in an expensive neighborhood because our child goes to school here.

And again:

My husband announced he was leaving, and then he tried to coerce me into letting him call 911 so he could commit me to a psych ward. After he left, I looked at his laptop and saw that he'd been applying for houses with his affair partner, who had left her daughters with their father and moved down here. Once she was settled, John was ready to go. She was his college crush, so now he's reliving his glory days.

And again:

I'm in the eye of the hurricane, or maybe the storm has passed. John left three months ago. Recognizing the degree of his mendacity has seared me. He'll never stop telling the lies that hold his ego together. I'm gobbling up old Hollywood noir movies because they seem so realistic. For my birthday I bought myself a hundred-year-old cast-iron skillet to replace the one John took with him. It arrives today.

The skillet arrived. I cooked dinner in it.

When I picked the child up the next day, I saw that John's house was freshly swept. A neat little package sat by the door, ready to be mailed.

John wouldn't have swept a floor or returned a package if I'd asked him to, but if he'd improved, he'd gone from the emotional age of three to four. *Look, Mama! I can do it myself!*

I asked him who'd been cleaning his house.

—*I have!*

—*Oh, so you do know how.*

—*Yeah. I just didn't clean before because you didn't like the way I did it.*

As if he were the first man ever to think of that.

After the child and I walked down to the rainbow lifeguard station in Venice one weekend, John started doing it with him regularly.

And after the child and I ordered some Japanese candy online, John signed up for a monthly Candies of the World package service—to insinuate himself into what the child and I did together, to poison it, or to claim it as his own.

Marni said that John would give up trying to be a real parent after a year or so. *He's trying hard now because all eyes are on him,* she said, *but he can't possibly sustain it.*

I baked the child an apple pancake and took him to the doctor for the insect bites he was still somehow getting almost daily.

At the doctor's office I called John and put him on speaker. He said that the child had had a few bites, but it wasn't a real problem. I hung up and just looked at the doctor. The child was covered in bites. The doctor prescribed a steroid cream and asked if I had a good lawyer.

I imagined John in a hospital bed, gaunt and jaundiced, dying, but I couldn't look at him and not feel his pain. I couldn't picture his body deteriorating and not feel it in my body even though he'd tried to manufacture a story that I was dangerous for my son to be around. I couldn't enjoy even the idea of his death, and it infuriated me. I prayed for an ice-cold heart.

Felix reported that Victoria hadn't seen their daughters in five months, not since she'd moved to California to fuck my husband.

The cat smelled my grief and stuck to me.

I figured out how to mount an adapter bar on my bike. Got the bar on the bike, the rack on the car, and the bike on the rack. I took a photo.

Felix wrote, *Victoria claims she didn't abandon our daughters, that she moved to California to be closer to our son, and that Covid travel restrictions have kept her from seeing the twins, but the children know that Victoria abandoned them without a thought as to how it would affect them. It's clear to them that their mother destroyed two families.*

When I told the mediator that Victoria hadn't just left her husband but also two of her children, she involuntarily sucked a breath past her teeth.

John would turn fifty in a few months, and he wanted a fresh start, far from any artists, surrounded instead by middle managers and the things that money can buy.

But at the moment, the child was covered in bug bites. I didn't know what to do. I'd already gotten him a new mattress. I rolled up his rug and put it in the back room. I didn't see a single bug.

I ordered a new rug and made tape slides of ten tiny black dots I found in his bedding. Two of them looked like mites; the rest were lint.

I ordered bird mite spray. The mites would be banished. The house would be tidy and clean and a site of healing.

Then I started getting bitten. The bites were as itchy as chigger bites.

Hannah said that John knew he was a piece of shit, but Marni said that John's justification was airtight. *He couldn't have done what he did if it wasn't,* she said.

Laundry, vacuum, exterminator. The pediatrician called in a topical cream to treat scabies in case the bird mite remediation failed.

I jogged a mile with the child.

John picked him up without speaking to me.

I felt deeply that I wasn't meant to have a partner.

But I'd had a partner for fourteen years.

But he wasn't a partner.

The exterminator said that fogging the house would kill everything from mites to rats and would cost three thousand dollars.

The child came home with new bites in his armpits.

I felt ready to lift a truck, but there was no truck to lift.

I picked up the scabies cream. I chose not to drive past John's house on the way home.

Hail science—the child's symptoms vastly improved after a single treatment.

Both John and Victoria then also needed to be treated for scabies.

I started on the kitchen cabinets and drawers. No more mystery stuff crammed into drawers and closets. Nothing extraneous, everything useful.

John had always needed to *see* everything all around him, glass jars of pasta taking up counter space and accumulating filth.

He'd wanted to see everything in order to know that it was there, that it existed, that he existed.

Then, once every bit of him was gone from the kitchen, his former domain, sadness came and crushed me.

The rage returned in the night. I got out of bed and did chores until I didn't even care if he died, until a neutral cloud surrounded the idea of him.

My parents remarked that I seemed happy for the first time in years.

Half the time the child was with his father. Half the time he was with me. Of that half, half of it was spent in school, and much of the rest of it was occupied by homework and activities. The interminable hours of toddlerhood were gone.

John had only ever placed the laundry near the hamper, and he'd only ever thrown something away in the trash by putting it at the very top of the bin, balancing it there, so that I'd have to push it in if I needed to throw anything else away, but since he'd left my bins filled slowly.

I unplugged the washing machine, disconnected the hoses, removed the mesh traps, and found the blockage—plastic bits from when John had washed a plastic-lined mat on a heavy cycle. I put it all back together and the thing worked.

Five months had passed.

On his first day home after a week with his father, the child shampooed his hair, flossed his teeth, washed his face, cleaned his ears, trimmed his nails, put his filthy sweater in the wash, and cried.

We bought smooth flat rocks at the masonry store and painted them for our new garden. I moved the pile of bricks to the side of the house because they were in the way, not because I thought it was time to stop throwing them.

I learned from an online video how to use my new drill. All the comments below it were grateful thanks from divorcées and widows.

I lay down in the child's bed before dinner. *Can I read to you?* he asked. He read to me from a children's poetry collection in his beautiful little voice, still a child's.

I felt more saturated with love for the child with every passing week, my capacity for it growing huger than I thought possible.

The number of times John said to the child during his check-in calls that he was *glad you and Mom had such a fun day* was proportional to his envy that we'd had a fun day.

On his check-in calls with John, the child told him about the Antarctica documentary we'd watched and the crafts we'd made. On his calls with me, he only ever told me about the video game he'd played all afternoon.

But then one night he told me that when he couldn't sleep, he liked to think about all of the animals from his video game.

I wrote to Naomi, the woman John cheated on and left, fourteen years ago, to be with me. I apologized to her for having believed that their relationship was over.

She wrote back that she'd never blamed me, only John.

I began to understand what a story is. It's a manipulation. It's a way of containing unmanageable chaos.

The job is to dredge it up, name it, and describe it completely.

After I scraped a concrete column pulling out of a parking space, instead of falling apart I said to the child, *Do you see all those stripes of paint on the column? Each one of those is from someone's car. People do this all the time.* Then I drove home, the headlights broken and the front bumper sagging.

In mediation, for the fourth time, John asked to reintroduce Victoria to the child right away, not to wait the year that we'd agreed upon. I said no, knowing that he'd immediately accede, wait a few more weeks, and then make the same request again as if for the first time, hoping for a different answer.

He seemed to have forgotten that when I asked him the same question over and over, he'd refused to answer and claimed that I was manipulating him.

A journalist came over to interview me for a feature about women writers who had children. Even though I wasn't attracted to him and would have been disgusted if I'd had to kiss him, having an unfamiliar cock in the house made me want to suck and fuck it.

I couldn't tell if the urge was entirely separate from my habit of locating any nearby need for emotional labor and immediately fulfilling it, but it didn't matter. Either way, when an entire civilization tells you that you owe that cock a good suck and fuck, it isn't a personal failure when you give in. You've been coerced.

One afternoon, the child and I saw John and Victoria at the gas station. They were cleaning the windows of Victoria's new car, poking each other with squeegees like teenagers, as in a movie or a nightmare. I was standing right behind them. Victoria looked shorter and broader than I remembered.

I said, *Hi, guys! Fancy meeting you here!* Victoria turned around and then looked sick and went to hide in the car. John slid over and said I'd received another health insurance reimbursement check at his house, and should he drop it off. He seemed to hope that a casual conversation would erase what the child and I had seen. *No, just put the mail in the school bag,* I cleanly replied.

John waved at the child in the backseat. He fogged up the window with his breath and wrote the child's name on it backward.

That night he had a check-in call.

—Dad, I know you're dating Victoria.

—I'm not dating Victoria! I was just hanging out with her.

Then he was quiet. His voice had cracked. Now we all knew. John calmed down and added, *That's adult stuff that you don't need to worry about,* but the damage was done.

At bedtime I told the child that Dad would probably never admit to lying. I told him that for months I hadn't known whether to tell him about Victoria. *You did the right thing,* the child said, hugging me.

My mother dubbed Victoria *John's gas station girl*.

During our next check-in call, the child showed me John's garden, bountiful as a nursery. John had made planters out of different colored woods. He was great at the beginnings of things, and for him, this was a big beginning, romancing a skilled gardener. Fourteen years earlier, he'd romanced me with all the compliments his writing teachers had given him during the degree program he didn't finish.

During John's next call, he asked the child, *What's the yummiest thing you ate today?*, which was a question I'd started asking him several weeks earlier. Then John whispered, *Dad loves Bear,* at the end of the call, which was also something I'd initiated. Did he think the child wouldn't notice?

Felix reported that the twins were visiting Victoria. John became very chatty, even sending me links to funny videos, which I ignored. He sent a long message about a work friend's heart attack, highlighting the fact that he was bringing food to the family and might have to take his check-in call from the road. I could smell his self-regard from miles away.

A few minutes later he texted again. The family had asked him not to bring the food, so he had a lot of take-out food in his *hot little hand,* a disgusting phrase he must have learned from Victoria. I responded, *No thx, we have stuff.*

I looked at photos of John from the beginning and saw his kind, gentle eyes. But they weren't the eyes of a kind man anymore. They were the eyes of a predator.

John had fucked Victoria in a hotel in August, and then he'd fucked me in October, for the last time, and then I'd had a yeast infection for several days that I'd ascribed to running in tight shorts, though I'd always run in tight shorts.

They probably hadn't used a condom. Or maybe they had, and the yeast had come from Victoria's drunk sugary mouth.

When my son was tiny, his frame of reference for identifying shapes and objects had initially been small, as everyone's is. He'd been interested in lightbulbs, and he'd noticed the shape of them everywhere. *Like a lightbulb,* he'd managed to say, accurately, almost daily, and once I'd been betrayed, I saw everywhere the signs I'd missed when it had been my turn. Half of my friends' marriages suddenly appeared to be on the cusp of shattering. I felt clairvoyant.

I moaned to Hannah that I'd made the wrong choice, that I should have been smarter.

We don't choose our lovers! Hannah said, almost angrily. *Our bodies do! Heterosexuality is for making babies!*

—*But you're with a man and aren't having any more babies!*

—*But my body doesn't know that!*

In the *Inferno,* Dante didn't punish the adulterers for what their bodies did; he punished them for claiming that their sin lay outside the realm of choice and therefore wasn't immoral. He punished them for breaking the promises they'd made on their wedding days.

I still tried to tell the story to anyone who would listen, in bits and pieces, with no sense of it as a story.

I looked through our wedding photos and found forty pictures that included Victoria. In several of them, she and John are sitting together and looking at me. Her décolletage is sunburned and her arms are flabby. She looks matronly.

I'd invested my time and sacrificed years of my career to a person whose next lover had haunted our marriage, who'd lingered on the edges of our wedding photos like an understudy.

I went for a walk. It took six miles to stop visualizing Victoria being hit by a car.

I was still surprised by how bodily the betrayal felt, how essentially private, like childbirth.

Initially I'd thought I'd put my life on hold for someone who had never fully considered me, but it was worse than that. John hadn't just been dismissing me. He'd been punishing me for my success.

I'd rewritten his secret autobiography, in which I was supposed to be the great man's wife. He'd never forgive me for that.

All the nights I'd stayed awake past my usual bedtime, when John had expressed concern, it wasn't concern for my insomnia. He'd just wanted to have phone sex with Victoria.

John called the child from his car, on his way to or from Victoria's apartment. He sounded distracted. When I heard him say good night to the child I heard a desperate liar on the verge of giving up.

Was I angry only because I'd chosen someone who would always be less intelligent, less successful? Had I done what men do when they marry beautiful, compliant idiots?

At my mammogram the receptionist asked me, *Is John Bridges still your emergency contact?* and I said no, and then I couldn't think of another person, so I wrote down Hannah's name even though she lived across the country.

When John arrived to fetch the child, he said, *It comes in waves*. Why was he describing this as a natural disaster when he alone had engineered it?

John's college friends had always been so careful with me, detached and polite, probably because they'd been drenched in stories of my insanity and possibly even believed John's tall tale about my institutionalization. They hadn't wanted to light any of my delicate fuses.

It must have been disturbing to watch me shatter. Some people had needed to comfort themselves that the shattering would be over soon and that it wasn't contagious.

Twelve years earlier, during our honeymoon, John had woken me one night to see the deer crunching their little hooves in the sand at our beachside cabin. *Wake up!* he'd said. *Deer! Beach deer!*

Whenever he'd told the story to someone else, he'd acted out the part of me waking up blearily, more sedated than I'm sure I sounded. Over the years his impersonation grew more contemptuous. *What? WHAT?* He made me sound like someone waking up from a coma, and then he'd add that I took medication that made me pass out every night. He'd say it with a sneer.

Did he have me confused with the lunatic he told everyone I was?

My psychiatric hospitalization had taken place seven years before I met him. I hadn't hidden it; in fact I spoke about it openly.

Somehow in the ensuing years that hospitalization had twisted, under the influence of John's contempt, into *institutionalization*. Not just that, but *willing institutionalization*. As if that were worse than a forced hold. As if you had to be extra crazy if you chose to accept treatment. As if admitting it were the craziest thing of all. As if people finding out about your craziness would be the most shameful disgrace imaginable. *Bipolar medication and willing institutionalization.*

The word. *Bipolar.* Which never was my official diagnosis—it was some subcategory of depression—but the word had been John's comfort. It was proof that I was sick and he wasn't, and that he was better than I was. *Bipolar medication.* He didn't seem to understand that all kinds of psychotropics treat all kinds of mood disorders. He seemed to think that my vials of pills, which I'd never hidden but kept on my night table, ought to be marked *XXX BIPOLAR XXX*, like bottles of hooch in old cartoons.

Our relationship had been a fourteen-year conversation about the intersection of mental health and art, but really it was two arguments that never touched: John's twin insistences that he was a great artist and that I was a deranged lunatic.

I'd never felt I needed to insist I was a great artist. You publish a book, you have some regrets, they subside, you write the next book. Sometimes I felt crazy, but who doesn't?

After his mother died, John had sneered at me that he had a reason to be depressed, and if you have a reason to be depressed, you don't need medication for it.

It was as fruitless to argue with him then as it was at the dinner party where he told everyone that we never had sex because I took sedative drugs at night. Not because I slept an unusually long time, or because my sleep was irregular; it was simply because I took medicine. He tried to present it as a logistical problem, that I was always asleep when he wanted to have sex, but I slept from eleven to seven every day, and he could have fucked me outside those hours. It was such an inane argument that I'd decided it couldn't possibly be happening. I pretended it wasn't.

And once I forgot all about it, I just kept on wondering how I might persuade my husband to fuck me. I thought of it as a problem I could solve all by myself.

I'm only going to do this once, John had solemnly said a few days before we were married.

On our wedding day I'd known I was taking a chance, and that we loved each other, and that we both had flaws that probably wouldn't ever disappear, and that our love could overpower those flaws.

There are no assurances, he'd solemnly said, months later.

The prospect of dying while knowing that you are loved, in the company of the other—that's the marriage vow. The core experience of spousal betrayal is having that happy scene torn away from you.

But dying alone, cradled by the universe, continuous with the rest of its energy, wasn't something I dreaded anymore. Worse things had already happened.

John hadn't hidden who he was in the beginning: insecure and envious, but also rapturous and admiring. In the beginning he'd seemed to admire and support me. When my career outpaced his, he'd tried to bury it under the story that I was crazy. He'd stopped talking about his insecurity about five years before he left, and I'd thought it had disappeared.

Maybe the trouble was simply that men hate women.

John had been trying to break up with Naomi for two months, he'd said, soon after we'd met and almost immediately started fucking.

Six months later, I'd been at his place on New Year's Eve. Our first new year together. A coq au vin was simmering in the oven. Naomi called, and John talked with her from the bathroom, with the door shut. When he got off the phone, he said he had to bring her some soup because she was sick. I waited for him for three hours.

The coq au vin was a holdover from his relationship with Naomi; she was from Bordeaux, and he'd learned to cook French dishes to impress her.

Fourteen years later, after he left me I never asked him to bring me soup and never reached out to him except for some perfunctory issue relating to child care. I never asked him to come back or perform anything that resembled apology or love.

A wedding vow is a mind game. You have to guess whether the person currently on his best behavior will someday value your physical, emotional, and financial health above the convenience of being able to just break the contract.

This guessing game can't be done with any degree of success. It's not even a guessing game. It's a coin toss. You're basing a lifelong plan on the behavior of a person who might change, or change back, to someone else.

A wedding vow is unlike other legal declarations in that there's no penalty for breaking it.

John's betrayal was a gift. My last bits of romantic silliness, all burned away.

I taught the child his father's new home address, which in nine months his father had never thought to do.

My denial phase lasted fifteen seconds, I praised myself, but then I remembered that it had lasted more than fourteen years.

I texted Marni, *I feel embarrassed about having been tricked by an idiot.*

She wrote back, *John changed all the rules without you knowing, which is the only way he could have tricked you. But he only tricked you a little. Remember that you suggested therapy, he said no, and you let him go in about fifteen sec-*

onds. You were already living quite capably without any input from him, and in fact while being actively sabotaged constantly.

Sick and delirious from Covid, six months before John left, I'd emailed him the track list for my funeral, just in case.

He'd slept downstairs on the sofa while I'd quarantined in bed, and that week he talked to Victoria on the phone for almost six hundred minutes.

Romance is nothing but a cheap craft-store decoration made to sanitize a desire to fuck.

Is that what marriage is for?

Is that what my marriage was for?

Almost a year later, the callus under my ring finger well flattened, I thought of John's mother. *Isn't she disappointed and ashamed? Isn't she going to speak to him and prevent all this from happening?*

And then I remembered that she was dead, and had been dead almost ten years. And then I was surprised that I thought of this man's mother as the strongest available check on his behavior. And I realized I'd always thought of him as a child, a spoiled little son.

It's time to stop finding deficits endearing, Marni said.

After dropping the child at school, I drove his sparring gear to his father's house, as planned. Victoria's car was in the driveway. I rang the bell three times and then banged on the door. John answered the door in a towel and a whisper. *Oh, the sparring gear,* he said, sounding embarrassed and surprised. I handed him the bag, all business. Then I walked back to the car and realized that John had made me ring the bell and bang on the door so I'd appear crazy.

At the belt test, the child was the highest belt in the room. I sat next to John, who had tied the child's belt wrong, and mid-test I had to run up to the mats and retie the belt, after which the other parents in the audience jokingly applauded me. Their children were white belts. They had no idea what it was to have attended five belt tests. They had no idea what it was to be divorced.

John leaned over at least half a dozen times to whisper to me during the test. I don't remember a thing he said except for the last thing, which was, *I forgot the fucking sparring gear*. I told him to drive home and get it and he said there was no time and then said, *I'm sure they have sparring gear that he can use,* and I said nothing more but silently communicated, without looking at him, without moving a muscle, that I was disappointed but not surprised. Which he knew. Which was why he'd left me.

But all through the test I took glances at his body and found it pleasing, despite everything, which is how I imagine men feel about women. I despised him and wished he would die so that he could no longer disappoint our child, and I still liked to look at his body.

John had probably told Victoria we'd already broken up. He'd probably told the story so well, so convincingly, that he'd come to believe it was true. And so he'd probably entered into his new relationship feeling clean and ready, just as he must have entered into our relationship after leaving confused, heartbroken Naomi.

I sorted my jar of foreign coins and found the Korean won John had brought home from his trip years earlier. When he dropped off the child's forgotten jacket the next day, I let the coins fall into a neat stack in his hand. He recoiled and dropped them all over the front stoop and said, *Sorry, I don't know why I just shivered there.* But he knew why.

A husband might be nothing but a bottomless pit of entitlement. You can throw all your love and energy and attention down into it, and the hole will never fill.

A nuclear family can destroy a woman artist. I'd always known that. But I'd never suspected how easily I'd fall into one anyway.

Years ago, when we'd picked the child up at preschool together, John had roared and roared and pretended to chase the tiny kids around the play yard. *Monster, monster!* they'd gleefully squeaked. One of the teachers had said to John, *They're going to remember this. They're old enough to remember.* But they won't remember that he did it only to feed off their adoration.

I wrote down the story again:

The child kept a pair of his father's eyeglasses on his night table for weeks. Then one day he threw them away.

A few weeks before John left, I'd taken out the trash and found the whole alley papered with yearbooks, letters, faded Polaroids, children's drawings, prayer cards, concert tickets from a 1987 performance of *Jesus Christ Superstar*. I'd gathered it all up, thought I should hide it, at least, from the prying eyes of—who pries in alleys? I didn't know, but I'd felt as if I'd found a naked body.

I'd picked everything up, every little paper clip and bead. There was a real estate license, long expired. It was an uncommon name. I'd found her on the internet and left a voicemail, and she'd called me back, and she'd said she'd pick up her things soon.

She'd used the phrase *my son's father* and I'd thought, not for the first time, *What a sad phrase. I'm so glad I never have to use it.*

Then John had left. I'd called her back and left another message. I'd said that my husband was divorcing me and that I had to leave. I hadn't had to leave, but I couldn't deal with her things in the house. There was too much going on.

When she came to pick up her things, she'd said, *What you did for me is amazing*. She said she'd pray for me. I trusted that God would listen.

I finally got the landlord to finish replacing the old drain-pipes. Finally all the drains worked. When we'd first moved in, the tub never really drained for more than a day or two after the handyman snaked it.

When I washed my hair, a light brown coin of it, rimmed in white suds, would collect at the drain. A few minutes later, after the rest of the water drained, a second, smaller coin would form. After brushing my teeth I'd pick out the second coin of hair and throw it away.

But when the tub drained ever slower, day by week by month, I left the second coin to form all by itself. And the next day, when it was time for me to shower—I got up first to feed the cat and feed the kid and make his lunch and get him ready for school while my husband texted with his girlfriend in Calgary—I saw that the wet little oval of hair had been dragged up the side of the tub the day before and left there, accusatory.

Look at your filth, my husband said silently, with that little ring of hair. *It's too disgusting for me to pick up and throw away.*

By the time he left me, he hadn't cleaned a bathroom in ten years.

I wrote, *Today this is as long as I can stand to think about it.*

My god, how I'd loved thinking about our long marriage. I'd loved thinking of myself as having the capacity for mature love, which I'd experienced as self-erasure and processed as achievement.

I thought of us walking together, a little bent, bony, stepping carefully, in our very old age, our gnarled hands clasped. His eyes are still a shocking green. Our hair is white. We walk together like people who have had fifty years to learn each other's gaits and to learn how to respond to each other's slight teeterings on the pavement. That future was gone. The image of it scraped at me.

But I'd only ever pictured that image from the perspective of someone watching the old couple, even though in the image I am supposedly the wife.

So I wasn't mourning an experience of being that wife; I was mourning a romantic image of her, walking with her beloved and adoring husband, who had never existed.

It was just a schmaltzy movie, a bathetic trigger for the romantic feelings, forged in my teens, that still lurked within me.

Back in my teens, when my first boyfriend had told me he wanted to break up, I'd cried, and he looked confused. *I was told to treat you like shit until you broke up with me,* he'd said, as if expecting credit for choosing the kinder option.

Marni wrote, *I've come to terms with the fact that I was disallowed from feeling my own success for years because my husband needed an average woman. When that was no longer possible, he went out and found one.*

Days before John had informed me our marriage was over, I was still saying, multiple times per day, non sequitur, *I love Mumbun!* per our old custom.

We'd only ever used each other's names when we were furious at each other.

He never said *Mumbun* again after he left, and neither did I. He backslid a few times to calling me *M,* but I never responded in kind.

I'd thought it would be hard, that I'd forget, but I didn't forget.

Years earlier, after our engagement, I'd wondered if I should change my surname to Bridges. I'd loved the idea of wearing a disguise, of submitting to wifehood in the world, and of being secretly free, but I was afraid to change my legal name because then I'd have to remember to sign checks with one name and books with a different name. I'd worried that I'd have to maintain two signatures and always be vigilant to use the correct one. That I'd feel like a liar. And so I'd decided to wait until we were married five years, and change my name then.

We clocked five years, but I didn't feel ready.

Then we clocked ten years, and I still didn't feel ready.

And then, five months after I gave John the steel spoon, it was over, and I didn't have to change my name back.

Before all that, when we were still a family, we celebrated holidays at the home of John's childhood friend Gail, who had taken her husband's name. They worked in corporate offices, drove luxury cars, and took their children to theme parks.

In late summer, a few months before leaving, John had suddenly needed to visit Gail. She was freaking out and needed to talk. The problem was vague, but Covid quarantine had been hard on everyone. I let him go and take care of his friend.

Weeks later, the last time we got together with Gail and her family, we'd gone to the beach. The kids splashed and played. Gail and her husband had known by then that John was about to leave me.

At least we'll never be that bad, I used to think when I'd heard stories like that, back when I was married.

Covid quarantine made it impossible for millions of cheaters to maintain their double lives. That whole first year, people kept telling me stories exactly like mine.

Then I became the story that other married people got off on, murmuring together in bed, pitying me, loving John for making them look good, cherishing every disgusting detail.

A year had passed, and all through the year, I hadn't wanted to tell John anything, and I hadn't wanted to ask him anything beyond the most basic mundanities.

And it occurred to me that I ought to be grateful to him for having successfully engineered that easy transition. By hating me.

John gave me a jar of homemade marmalade with a custom-printed label on top. *Bridges Farms.* To distinguish it from the handwritten-with-Sharpie labeling we used to do together. To show how he was better then, without me, showing that he could be a better wife than I ever was, plus be the husband.

He tried to make it look easy, to show me that he could do what I did without even trying, to throw in my face all fourteen years of all the invisible work I did.

Marni told me that John had shown her his paintings once, and that I'd stepped in and out of the garage studio to remind him that he needed to do something. When I'd left, John had rolled his eyes in front of her, expecting her to commiserate.

Hannah told me that at one of my book launches, years earlier, she'd had some wine and, feeling jolly, asked John if he was excited about my new book. *She's really, really nervous. She hates readings,* he'd said, sounding annoyed.

It disgusted me, under normal circumstances, to think about shit going anywhere except a sewer or a hole in the ground, but during the first weeks after John left, I'd fantasized about shitting in my hand and smearing and packing the shit into the backs of all of his paintings—the ones he'd photographed and sent to his gallerist, who'd never responded.

Betrayal is primitive and elemental, and deep in the memory of my body an old, animal knowledge had stirred to life.

Years ago I'd sat next to a single woman at a dinner party. I'd worried that John was seated between two famous people and felt small. I'd told my seatmate that I thought John was amazing, hoping that my assurances would find their way through the room, somehow, and make their way to my husband's ego.

I'd wanted it both ways: I wanted the normal people to recognize me as successful, having married and procreated and maintained a nuclear family; and I'd wanted the weirdos, too, to recognize me, hiding in my normie costume. I wanted to have and eat my cake.

When I read those three months of his text messages, I saw that he'd always sent Victoria links to the funny online things I sent him. I wondered if there was a point at which he thought, *I'll stay married for a while longer, since my wife gives me links to funny online things that my girlfriend likes.*

Felix said that John's friends had thought I was too good for him, and that John had always explained that I was profoundly unstable, deeply crazy, and had even been hospitalized.

Imagine having to explain to your friends that your wife is with you only because there's something wrong with her.

After John left, I swept out the garage and discovered that he could, in fact, receive my calls and texts in his garage studio. He'd always claimed there was no reception.

A few months before he left, he'd called me out to the garage and asked me for a critique of a new painting. I'd sandwiched the critique in praise. *Well, that's just wrong,* he'd quickly said to the criticism.

The only lie I'd ever told my husband was that a piece of glass left over from a DIY project had cracked on its own, and not because I'd dropped it. It had felt like a neutralizing decision. It had felt like getting even with the harm he'd done me. It had felt like a drop in the bucket of that harm.

Which is, of course, exactly how he'd felt about his lying and cheating.

How large was his bucket? What else was in it, besides Victoria?

I wrote down the story again:

As soon as we got settled and I found an adjunct-teaching job, John would lose his job and we'd move again. The more untethered and dependent and overwhelmed I grew, the surer he felt that he should be the one making decisions about where to live, since he was, by that point, bringing in most of the money.

I believed him, especially when he added that I was crazy, since, after all, I'd been hospitalized that one time.

Calling a woman crazy is a man's last resort when he's failed to control her.

But wait—*was* I crazy?

When John had wanted to hang a pull-up bar in a doorway of our first California house, I'd refused to let him because I feared I'd be tempted to hang myself from it.

When our son had disappeared at the beach and we'd had the lifeguards scouring the sand, I'd stood and said, *Oh my god oh my god* loudly enough that people were staring, and I hadn't cared. I took a break from my keening to inform my stonily silent husband that if the child were dead, I would kill myself.

But the child was found, and I didn't kill myself.

That's the problem with women like us, Marni said. *We don't die. When I tell people I look forward to dying, they don't get it. I'm just fucking tired. I'm not going to kill myself, but I'm ready to rest. When I went on vacation I went snorkeling and couldn't move. The current was too strong. But it was just beautiful underwater. I thought, Well, if this is it, it's not bad. Then the stupid boat guide saved me and gave me a hundred bucks.*

I closed my eyes and gathered the entire marriage into a pile. It looked like a scene from a building demolition, rebar and jagged wood, half a lifetime's worth of stuff. Then I compacted it and the pile contracted, crushed by heavy machines. When I was done, it was black as coal and had the density of a collapsed star. I opened my eyes.

A year after he left, I felt a stirring of awareness: Maybe he'd known he'd needed to let me go so I could be free to do my work and live my life, and maybe on some deep, secret level, it was an act of duty and kindness.

But that's just me projecting a pretty moral onto a story of deliberate harm. When I was a wife, that was my main job.

When I arrived at John's house, the child was eating cereal out of a beautiful blue bowl. I recognized the brand and looked it up on the internet. The bowl had cost forty-four dollars.

He'd left me the blue bowls I'd bought at Target, years before we met. I couldn't have spent more than ten bucks for the set.

John's new house was full of new expensive things. Those bowls, the leather sofa, the custom-framed pictures—he'd bought all of it quickly, before we'd split what was left of our savings.

In the beginning, every time John and I had heard about an affair, we used to say that it sounded exhausting to carry on like that, to tell so many lies, take care of two relationships, make time for phone calls and trysts. I really had felt that way, and since John was so lazy in the rest of his life, I'd assumed he'd felt that way, too.

A month before he left, Victoria had written to him: *Imagine these words coming straight out of my mouth and into yours. And then my mouth going somewhere else . . . How much longer before we can celebrate?*

I hadn't had any trouble masturbating after John left. But after more than a year, while rubbing myself in bed, I saw him suddenly hanging there, looking down at me with that calm green gaze. I was surprised; it was the first time that had happened. The rage had left my body, and the rest of the feelings were finding their way back in.

The smell of a woman's cunt on her own fingers, I wrote in my notebook that night. It felt important.

Everything I'd written during the marriage belonged to John and me equally, since California was a community property state. But everything afterward was mine.

The intellectual property I'd created during the life of the marriage was considered shared property in the eyes of the law, so even though John earned hundreds of thousands of dollars more than I did, every year for the rest of the settlement I'd have to pay him half of what I earned from four of my books. He could have let me keep the money, but he didn't. I tried to forget about it. I couldn't change the law if I wanted to, and it might work the other way, if some cheater wrote a hit movie while he was married. In their divorce, his chump wife would benefit. I tried to feel that scenario balancing mine.

During a five-minute break in my online lecture I checked my email and found a message from the mediator with the subject heading *Final Judgment*. Adrenaline surged into my throat. I couldn't open it; I had two more hours to teach onscreen.

I wondered if John felt the same strange dread at suddenly being divorced, but of course he didn't; he was already several years into his next relationship.

Days later, I felt my mind start to allocate space to things other than the divorce. Those other things, as they made their way into my awareness—music, a squirrel in a tree, the sun and sky—felt new and unspoiled, as if I'd never thought about them before.

For a long time I'd thought of marriage as something I was good at, and that each wedding anniversary was an achievement. I was good at absorbing abuse. I'd been good at playing the piano, too, but after I'd quit I felt the same relief.

John and I opened new bank accounts and traded account numbers. John didn't know how to read the account number on the bottom of his new checks and sent me a photo of a check so I could read it for him, but I didn't do it to help him. I did it so that I didn't have to deal with it later on, after some financial transaction failed.

The tide was high and the sand was hell to walk through, wet and loosely packed, but I dragged myself a mile down the beach so the child could watch the surf beat the rocks. On the way back a dog chased him and he cried. My back and neck seized up. But then there were dolphins.

There were so many perspectives on those fourteen years, and each one was newly, separately instructive. Once I could stand looking at it from one direction, I discovered another and had to figure everything out all over again.

Early on, maybe five years in, John had said, *Are you only with me because I'm dark and handsome?* and I'd said, *I've left darker and handsomer,* which had been true. But I saw now that it had also been a dodge. Even then, I'd known I was drawn mainly to his body.

Maybe a man's relationship to another person is only ever adversarial.

Almost two years had passed, and whatever it was that I hadn't gotten over, I wasn't sure I wanted to get over it if the prize was having to take on a husband again.

John had taught me a lesson that felt indelible: that there are no assurances. That anyone might do anything to anyone.

Maybe I should have followed my instinct, years back, when I'd yearned to move to a little house upstate, all alone.

While we waited for the child to put his shoes on, John stood in my living room, preeningly explaining something, polishing his sunglasses on the bottom of his shirt, exposing a good six inches of belly, which was noticeably doughier than it had been a year ago. Its hairs were long and straggly. I tried not to look at it.

John had always rubbed his eyes when he was excited about explaining something, about showing his authority. The gesture never varied. When he started rubbing his eyes I immediately got bored.

When you're a liar, you always know something that other people don't know. Maybe lying to me made John feel extra smart.

Everything he did to me, all the lying—he'd thought he was avenging a wound I'd inflicted on purpose. He must have felt like a guttering candle, on the verge of being extinguished.

Victoria's attention affirmed to him that he existed, that he was important, that he was worth everything, even her family. Even his family. Imagine how good that must have felt.

Next to Victoria, John didn't look like a failed artist or a faithless husband. He looked like a guy who was valuable enough to make someone throw away a twenty-five-year marriage.

Someday John's contempt would find its way into that romance, too, but it was no concern of mine.

Now I stand in the shade of a tree.

Someone has left three perfect walnut halves on the lowest branch. Perhaps a lucky squirrel will find them. The child steps over them and keeps going up. The light in the sky is fading.

I'm not thinking about John. He isn't part of this.

I am in a park, which is a wordless place.

I'm looking at a tree with a child in it, my child, who has come out of my body and gone calmly and happily up a tree. I'm looking up at him, watching over him from underneath.

My marriage is done. The last artifact of it is in the tree now. I feel like myself.

The child sits up high and considers the park from the highest comfortable seat.

It's as if I've deployed him.

The boy in the tree looks down at the world.

He's the engine by which I learn what is left of my life.

I remember how desperately I had to cling to the story of my happy marriage. It took effort. It felt so good to stop lying.

At karate this afternoon I sit with an unfamiliar woman who usually brings her daughter to practice on a different day. We talk about how good it was for our kids to have the dojo, even online, during the long quarantine. I hear myself say, *My husband and I divorced this past year, and the consistency and community were just so good for our child.*

No alarm bells ring; no flames flicker. A moment later, she and I are talking about something else.

ACKNOWLEDGMENTS

I wish to thank Parisa Ebrahimi and PJ Mark above all others, and to acknowledge the generous support of Paige Ackerson-Kiely, Jim Behrle, Sam Chapman, Jean Connolly, J. D. Daniels, Elizabeth Doan, Amy Fusselman, Garry Gekht, Makenna Goodman, Andrew Sean Greer, Daniel Handler, Sheila Heti, James Kent, Jennifer L. Knox, Diane Kramer, Catherine Lacey, Erinn Lalezari, Tanya Larkin, Irene Lusztig, Frank Manguso, Judith Manguso, Jenny Moore, Mary Mount, Ted Mulkerin, Leigh Newman, Julie Orringer, Ed Park, Christa Parravani, Bobbie Poledouris, Alexa de los Reyes, Karen Gaul Schulman, Leanne Shapton, Eleanor Skimin, Susan Steinberg, Amanda Stern, Caeli Wulfson Widger, Antoine Wilson, the teams at Hogarth and Janklow & Nesbit—and especially Tracy Schorn and the life-saving community of Chump Nation.

Parts of this book were included, in slightly different forms, in "Love," included in *Pets: An Anthology* (Tyrant Books, 2020), edited by Jordan Castro.

ABOUT THE AUTHOR

SARAH MANGUSO is the author of eight previous books, including the novel *Very Cold People* and several works of nonfiction and poetry. Her work has been recognized by a Guggenheim Fellowship and the Rome Prize. She lives in Los Angeles.

sarahmanguso.com

ABOUT THE TYPE

This book was set in Fairfield, the first typeface from the hand of the distinguished American artist and engraver Rudolph Ruzicka (1883–1978). Ruzicka was born in Bohemia (in the present-day Czech Republic) and came to America in 1894. He set up his own shop, devoted to wood engraving and printing, in New York in 1913 after a varied career working as a wood engraver, in photoengraving and banknote printing plants, and as an art director and freelance artist. He designed and illustrated many books and was the creator of a considerable list of individual prints—wood engravings, line engravings on copper, and aquatints.